There is a splat-splat of naked footsteps in the mud and a girl child of about fifty or so seasons squirms under the awning, looking fearfully over her shoulder for any signs of pursuit as she does so.

Your eyes, as sharp as an owl's in the gloom, pick out her scrawny form and the squalid, torn and muddied sackcloth tunic, inadequate protection against the cold of the night. She cannot see in the gloom and she begins to sob quietly, oblivious of your presence.

Gamebooks from Fabled Lands Publishing

by Jamie Thomson and Dave Morris:

Fabled Lands 1: The War-Torn Kingdom
Fabled Lands 2: Cities of Gold and Glory
Fabled Lands 3: Over the Blood-Dark Sea
Fabled Lands 4: The Plains of Howling Darkness
Fabled Lands 5: The Court of Hidden Faces
Fabled Lands 6: Lords of the Rising Sun

by Dave Morris:

Heart of Ice
Down Among the Dead Men
Necklace of Skulls
Once Upon a Time in Arabia
Crypt of the Vampire
The Temple of Flame
The Castle of Lost Souls

by Oliver Johnson:

Curse of the Pharaoh
The Lord of Shadow Keep

by Jamie Thomson and Mark Smith:

Way of the Tiger 1: Avenger
Way of the Tiger 2: Assassin
Way of the Tiger 3: Usurper

In preparation:

Way of the Tiger 4: Overlord
Way of the Tiger 5: Warbringer
Way of the Tiger 6: Inferno

Way of the Tiger
USURPER!

JAMIE THOMSON
& MARK SMITH

Originally published 1985 by Knight Books
This edition published 2014 by Fabled Lands Publishing
an imprint of Fabled Lands LLP

www.sparkfurnace.com

Illustrations by Hokusai, Aude Pfister, Mylène Villeneuve,
Dominique Gilis, Maria Nikolopoulou and Antoine Di Lorenzo

Irsmuncast map by Leo Hartas

Edited by Richard S. Hetley

With thanks to Mikaël Louys, Michael Spencelayh, Paul Gresty,
David Walters and John Jones of Project Aon

ISBN-13: 978-1-909905-12-2
ISBN-10: 1909905127

WARNING!

Do not attempt any of the techniques or methods described in this book. They could result in serious injury or death to an untrained user.

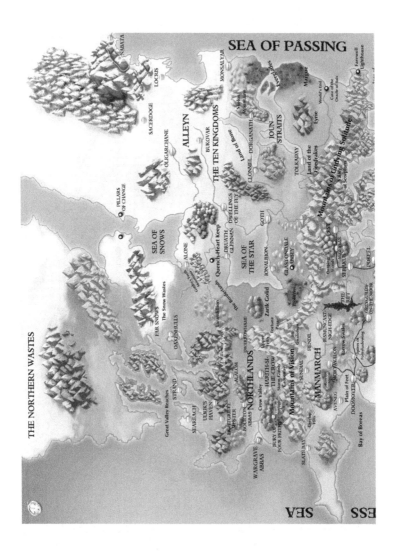

ENDLESS

Bay of Boreas
DOOMOVER
HORNGROTH
MOTHER
Desolation of the Serpent
TOR
Desert of the Aggrieved
STRAKAAN
HOY
Island of the Goddess
SEA ELVES' SOUND

Mountains of Horn
Land of Beasts
GREYDAWN
WALL OF SHADOW
Spires of Foreshadowing
GLENGARTHS-ON-THE-MOOR
GREAT PLAIN
Dheryan Mountains
Dhervan Desert
Irhal Plain
BESSARABIAN
TIMET
GYNDERENE
UPANISHAD
SOUTHLANDS

POMEEL
Great South Road
ANTIOCHUS

KETTLENE
VINTOMEN
Red Desolation
NOWAKI
Hungry Plain
LEMBROB

JUNGLE OF KHESH
SCELON
Scorpion Hills
Beggar's Bund

Hunting Plain
Desert of the Forsaken
NAPOL
PORT OF REAVERS
SEA OF SZEGED
Desert of the Oracle

HEARTSEA
ASANTI HOMELANDS
HEARTGUARD
YARBOL

UTTELENDE
The Lands of No Return

INNER SEA
Isle of Thieves
HAVEN OF TOR
Fangs of Nadir
ELEMENTAL SEA
Island of Ouroboros

FOREST OF FABLES
Greenfield River

Jaws of Forgetfulness
Farewell Lighthouse

DRAGONHOLD

To the Island of Plenty and the Island of Tranquil Dreams

100 MILES

THE WAY OF THE
TIGER

Orb Map by Aude Pfister
Copyright © 2013 Megara Entertainment.
All rights reserved. Layout: Mikaël LOUYS

Adventure Gamebooks

Ninja Character Sheet

Combat Ratings								
Punch	O							
Kick	O							
Throw	O							
Fate Modifier	O							

Skills	+ Shurikenjutsu

NINJA TOOLS

NINJA COSTUME

BREATHING TUBE

IRON SLEEVES

GAROTTE

FLASH POWDER

FLINT & TINDER

SPIDERFISH

BLOOD OF NIL

Endurance

Inner Force

STARTS AT 20	STARTS AT 5

SPECIAL ITEMS

# of Shuriken

Notes

STARTS AT 5

Winged Horse Kick

Leaping Tiger Kick

1

2

Forked Lightning Kick

Iron Fist Punch

Tiger's Paw Punch

Cobra Strike
Punch

Whirlpool Throw

Dragon's Tail Throw

Teeth of Tiger Throw

Adventure Gamebooks

<u>Opponent Encounter Boxes</u>

<u>Name:</u> <u>Endurance:</u>	<u>Name:</u> <u>Endurance:</u>	<u>Name:</u> <u>Endurance:</u>
<u>Name:</u> <u>Endurance:</u>	<u>Name:</u> <u>Endurance:</u>	<u>Name:</u> <u>Endurance:</u>
<u>Name:</u> <u>Endurance:</u>	<u>Name:</u> <u>Endurance:</u>	<u>Name:</u> <u>Endurance:</u>

BACKGROUND

On the magical world of Orb, alone in a sea that the people of the Manmarch call Endless, lies the mystical Island of Tranquil Dreams.

Many years have passed since the time when you first saw its golden shores and emerald rice meadows. A servant brought you, braving the distant leagues of the ponderous ocean from lands to which you have never returned. Your loyal servant laid you, an orphan, at the steps of the Temple of the Rock praying that the monks would care for you, for she was frail and dying of a hideous curse.

Monks have lived on the island for centuries, dedicated to the worship of their God, Kwon, He who speaks the Holy Words of Power, Supreme Master of Unarmed Combat. They live only to help others resist the evil that infests the world. Seeing that you were alone and needed care, the monks took you in and you became an acolyte at the Temple of the Rock. Nothing was made of the strange birthmark, shaped like a crown, which you carry on your thigh, though you remember that the old servant insisted that it was of mystical importance. Whenever you have asked about this the monks have bade you meditate and be patient.

The most ancient and powerful of them all, Naijishi, Grandmaster of the Dawn, became your foster-father. He gave you guidance and training in the calm goodness of Kwon, knowledge of men and their ways and how to meditate so that your mind floats free of your body and rides the winds in search of truth.

From the age of six, however, most of your time has been spent learning the Way of the Tiger. Now you are a ninja, a master of the martial arts and a deadly assassin who can kill the most powerful enemies unseen and unsuspected. Like a tiger, you are strong, stealthy, agile, patient in the stalking of prey and deadly. On the Island of Plenty and in the Manmarch the fabled ninja, known as the 'Men with no Shadow', are held in awe – the mere mention of ninja strikes fear into people's hearts. But you are one of the few who worship Kwon and follow the Way of the Tiger. You use your skill as a bringer of death to rid the world of evil-doers.

At an early age you hung by the hands for hours on end from the branches of trees to strengthen your arms. You ran for miles, your light-footed speed enough to keep a thirty-foot ribbon trailing above the ground. You trod tightropes, as agile as a monkey. Now you swim like a fish and leap like a tiger, you move like the whisper of the breeze and glide through the blackest night like a shade. Before he died, Naijishi taught you the Ninja's Covenant.

NINJA NO CHIGIRI

'I will vanish into the night; change my body to wood or stone; sink into the earth and walk through walls and locked doors. I will be killed many times, yet will not die; change my face and become invisible, able to walk among men without being seen.'

It was after your foster-father Naijishi's death that you began to live the words of the Covenant. A man came to the island, Yaemon, Grandmaster of Flame. Using borrowed sorcery he tricked the monks into believing that he was a worshipper of Kwon from the Greater Continent. He was indeed a monk but he worshipped Kwon's twisted brother, Vile, who helps the powerful to subdue the weak, and wicked men to rule fools. Yaemon slew Naijishi – no one could match him in unarmed combat – and he stole the Scrolls of Kettsuin from the Temple. Once more you knew the pain of loss for you had loved Naijishi as a father. You swore an oath to Kwon that one day you would avenge his death.

THE MALICE OF THE GODS OF EVIL

As chronicled in the books *AVENGER!* and *ASSASSIN!* you used your skills as a hunter and a bringer of death to avenge the killing of Naijishi, your spiritual father. You tracked his murderer, Yaemon, Grandmaster of the evil monks of the Scarlet Mantis, to Quench-heart Keep, in the shadow of the Goblin's Teeth Mountains. A Ranger, Glaivas, brought you across the sea on his ship, the *Aquamarin*, and you landed at the city of Doomover, in the Manmarch. You travelled hundreds of leagues through the wilderness, crossing the Mountains of Vision at Fortune Pass, where you were forced to kill Olvar the Chaos-Bringer, a berserk barbarian. Thence you journeyed to Druath Glennan and to Quench-heart Keep. Yaemon had stolen the Scrolls of Kettsuin which hold the secret to the word of power which would bind your god, Kwon, in Inferno. Two other powerful and evil men had joined him; each knew another such word of power, to bind a god or goddess in the lake of boiling blood for eternity.

In storm and darkness before the red moon, you took the life, or so you thought, of Yaemon, as well as Manse the Deathmage, a reverencer of Nemesis, the most powerful of the gods of evil, and Honoric, leader of the dreaded Legion of the Sword of Doom. With his dying breath as he lay drenched with rain and sweat at your feet, Yaemon told you that he killed your birth father whom you never knew. Then your god Kwon spoke to you, and you knew that you had been chosen by him to fulfil a glorious destiny for it may be that you will one day join him in the Garden of the Gods.

But the malice of the gods of evil beats down upon you still and your return to the Island of Tranquil Dreams was not an easy one. The trials of your journey are still fresh in your mind: your narrow escape from Quench-heart Keep; the desperate flight across the Manmarch and the terrible struggle with Mardolh, Son of Nil; your adventures on the Island of Plenty where you fought a great battle against the ninja that followed the Way of the Scorpion. There was great feasting and celebrating when at last you regained your homeland, the saviour of the lands of men. On the next day you rested, until the Grandfather of the Dawn came to your cell. He told you that Honoric still lived. 'He has sworn vengeance. He survived even the Blood of Nil, though he was near death for some days. Word has just reached us that the Legion of the Sword of Doom prepares once more for war.

'But enough of this; you cannot bear the cares of the world on your shoulders at all times. Come, there is little left that I can teach you, but what I can I will. Tomorrow I will tell you something that has been hidden from you. The time has come for me to tell you who your parents were, who you are, you who have become Avenger, the most deadly warrior of them all.'

RULES OF COMBAT

As a master of Taijutsu, the ninja's art of unarmed combat, you have four main ways of fighting: throwing shuriken (see under skills), kicks, punches and throws.

In general it will be harder to hit an opponent when kicking but a kick will do more damage than a punch. A throw, if successful, will allow you to follow up with a possible 'killing blow', but if you fail a throw your Defence against an opponent will be lower, as you are open to attack. Shuriken are a special case and will be mentioned in the text when you can use them.

Whenever you are in a combat you will be asked which type of attack you wish to make. See the Way of the Tiger illustrations for the different types of kicks, punches and throws available to you. Think about your opponent and its likely fighting style. Trying to throw a giant enemy is not going to be as easy as throwing an ordinary man, for example. You will be told which paragraph to turn to, depending on your choice.

When you are resolving combat, you will find it useful to record your opponent's current Endurance score. A number of Encounter Boxes are provided with your Character Sheet for this purpose.

The combats have been presented in such a way that it is possible for you to briefly examine the rules and begin play almost immediately, but fighting is tactical. Do not forget the rules for blocking and Inner Force (see below), as you will rarely be told when to use these in the text.

PUNCH
When you try to strike an enemy with a punch, that enemy will have a Defence number. You need to score higher than this number on the roll of two dice (an Attack Roll). You get to add your Punch Modifier (see below) to this roll. If the score is higher than his or her Defence number, you have punched your opponent successfully. In this case, roll one more die. The result is the amount of damage you have inflicted on your opponent. Every opponent has Endurance

or 'hit points'. The damage you do is subtracted from your opponent's Endurance total. If this has reduced your opponent's score to 0 or less, you have won.

Punch Modifier: Whenever you make an Attack Roll to determine whether or not you have successfully punched an opponent, add or subtract your Punch Modifier. This number reflects your skill in using the punches of the Way of the Tiger. Your starting Punch Modifier is 0, as noted on your Character Sheet. This may change during the adventure.

The Enemy's Attack: After you punch, any opponent still in the fight will counter attack. You will be given your Defence number. Roll two dice, and if the score is greater than your Defence, you have been hit. The amount of damage inflicted upon you depends on the opponent and will be noted in the text, in a format such as 'Damage: 1 Die + 1' or '2 Dice' or '1 Die + 2'. Simply roll the required number of dice and add any other number given. This is the total damage inflicted upon you. However, before you subtract this score from your Endurance, you may choose to try and block or parry the attack (see block) to prevent any damage.

KICK

The kick and the Kick Modifier work exactly as the punch, except that a kick will do 2 more points of damage than a punch ('1 Die + 2'). It will often be harder to hit with a kick. If the opponent survives, he or she will counter attack.

THROW

The throw and Throw Modifier work as the punch to determine success. A throw does no damage to your foe; instead, you will be allowed another attack, a punch or kick, with a +2 bonus to hit (like an extra Punch Modifier or Kick Modifier) and +2 to damage. (All bonuses are cumulative – a kick normally does '1 Die + 2' damage, so after a successful throw it does '1 Die + 4'.) The opponent will only counter attack against a throw if you fail.

ENDURANCE

You begin the game with 20 points of Endurance. Keep a running total of your Endurance on your Character Sheet. It will probably be the number that will change most as you are wounded, healed etc. When you reach 0 Endurance or less, you are dead and your adventure ends. When restoring Endurance, you cannot go above your maximum of 20.

BLOCK

As a ninja, a master of Taijutsu, you have the ability to block or parry incoming blows with various parts of your body, often your forearms. For this purpose, thin lightweight iron rods have been sewn into your sleeves enabling you to block even swords and other weapons. During combat, if you have been hit, you may try to block the blow and take no damage. Roll two dice. If the score is less than your Defence given in that combat, you have successfully blocked the blow, and take no damage. If your score is equal to or greater than your Defence, you take damage in the normal way. In any case, because you have taken the time to block, your next attack will be less effective, as your opponent has had more time to react. Whether your block is successful or not, −2 will be applied to your Punch, Kick and Throw Modifier for your next attack only. Remember, you can only block blows, not missiles or magic.

INNER FORCE

You begin the game with 5 points of Inner Force. Through meditation and rigorous training you have mastered the ability to unleash spiritual or inner power through your body in the same way as the karate experts of today break blocks of wood and bricks. In any combat, before you roll the dice to determine if you will hit or miss an opponent, you may choose to use Inner Force. If you do, deduct one point from your Inner Force score. This is used up whether or not you succeed in striking your opponent. If you are successful, however, double the damage you inflict – first make your roll for damage and add any bonus (e.g., '1 Die + 2' for a kick), then double the result. When your Inner Force is reduced to

0, you cannot use Inner Force again until you find some way to restore it – so use it wisely. When restoring Inner Force, you cannot go above your maximum of 5.

FATE

Luck plays its part and the goddess Fate has great power on the world of Orb. Whenever you are asked to make a Fate Roll, roll two dice, adding or subtracting your Fate Modifier. If the score is 7–12, you are lucky and Fate has smiled on you. If the score is 2–6, you are unlucky and Fate has turned her back on you. You begin your adventure with a Fate Modifier of 0. Later on, this might go up or down, as you are blessed or cursed by Fate.

NINJA TOOLS

As well as any equipment you may take depending on your skills (see next), as a ninja you have certain tools with you from the beginning. These are:

THE NINJA COSTUME

During the day you would normally be disguised as a traveller, beggar or suchlike. At night when on a mission, you would wear costume. This consists of a few pieces of black cloth. One piece is worn as a jacket covering the chest and arms, two others are wound around each leg and held in at the waist. Finally, a long piece of cloth is wrapped around the head, leaving only the eyes exposed. The reverse side of the costume can be white, for travel on snowy ground, or green, for travel in woods or grasslands.

IRON SLEEVES

Sewn into the sleeves of your costume are four thin strips of iron, the length of your forearm. These allow you to parry or block blows from swords and other cutting weapons.

BREATHING TUBE

Made from bamboo, this can be used as a snorkel allowing you to remain underwater for long periods of time. It can also be used as a blow-pipe in conjunction with the Poison Needles skill, for added range.

GARROTTE

A specialised killing tool of the ninja, this is a length of wire used to assassinate enemies by strangulation.

FLASH POWDER

This powder, when thrown in any source of flame, causes a blinding flash. You have enough for one use only.

FLINT AND TINDER

Used for making fires.

SPIDERFISH

Salted and cured, this highly venomous fish is used as a source for the deadly poison used in conjunction with the Poison Needles skill, and as a useful way of removing any guardian beasts or animals.

THE BLOOD OF NIL

You usually carry one dose of the most virulent poison known on Orb, but you have already used it in Book 2: *ASSASSIN!* This venom is extremely difficult and very dangerous to collect for it is taken from the barb of a scorpion son of the God, Nil, Mouth of the Void.

THE SKILLS OF THE WAY OF THE TIGER

You have been trained in ninjutsu almost all of your life. Your senses of smell, sight and hearing have been honed to almost superhuman effectiveness. You are well versed in woodcraft, able to track like a bloodhound, and to cover your own tracks. Your knowledge of plants and herb lore enables you to live off the land. You are at the peak of physical fitness, able to run up to 50 miles a day and swim like a fish. Your training included horsemanship, a little ventriloquism, meditation, the ability to hold yourself absolutely still for hours on end, perfecting your balance, and 'The Seven Ways of Going' or disguise. The latter skill involves comprehensive training so that you can perform as a minstrel, for instance, if this disguise is used. However, a major part of this training has been stealth, hiding in shadows, moving silently, and breathing as quietly as possible, enabling you to move about unseen and unheard. You begin the game with these skills.

There are nine other skills. One of these, Shurikenjutsu, is always taught to a ninja in training. This you must take, but you may then choose three other skills from the remaining eight, and note them on your Character Sheet.

SHURIKENJUTSU

You begin the adventure with five shuriken. The type you specialise in are 'throwing stars', small razor-sharp star-shaped disks of metal. You can throw these up to a range of about 30 feet with devastating effect. If you throw a shuriken, you will be given a Defence number for your target. Roll two dice, and if the score is higher than the Defence number, you will have hit your target. The text will describe the damage done. You may find yourself in a position where you are unable to retrieve a shuriken once you have thrown it. Keep a running total in the box provided on your Character Sheet, crossing off a shuriken each time you lose one. If you have none left, you can no longer use this skill. You are free to carry as many as you find in your adventures.

ARROW CUTTING

Requiring excellent muscular co-ordination, hand and eye judgment and reflexes, this skill will enable you to knock aside, or even catch, missiles such as arrows or spears.

ACROBATICS

The ability to leap and jump using flips, cartwheels, etc, like a tumbler or gymnast.

IMMUNITY TO POISONS

This involves taking small doses of virulent poisons over long periods of time, slowly building up the body's resistance. This enables you to survive most poison attempts.

FEIGNING DEATH

Requiring long and arduous training, a ninja with this ability is able to slow down heart rate and metabolism through will power alone, thus appearing to be dead.

ESCAPOLOGY

A ninja with this skill is able to dislocate the joints of the body and to maximise the body's suppleness, allowing movement through small spaces, and escape from bonds and chains by slipping out of them.

POISON NEEDLES

Sometime known as Spitting Needles, with this skill you can place small darts, coated with a powerful poison that acts in the blood stream, onto your tongue. By curling the tongue into an 'O' shape and spitting or blowing, the dart can be propelled up to an effective range of about 15 feet. A useful surprise attack, the source of which is not always perceptible.

PICKING LOCKS, DETECTING AND DISARMING TRAPS

The ability to open locked doors, chests etc. With this skill you would carry various lockpicks in the pockets of your costume, including a small crowbar or jemmy. You are also trained to notice traps and to use the lock-picking tools to disarm them.

CLIMBING

Comprehensive training in the use of a grappling hook and hand and foot clamps, or cat's claws. The padded four-pronged hook has forty feet of rope attached to it. Used to hook over walls, niches etc, allowing you to pull yourself up the rope. The cat's claws are spiked clamps, worn over the palm of the hands and the instep of the feet, enabling you to embed your claws into a wall and climb straight up like a fly, and even to crawl across ceilings.

SPECIAL RULES FOR THIS BOOK

If you have not played and successfully completed Book 2: *ASSASSIN!* in the Way of the Tiger series then you begin this book with the equipment listed. If you have successfully completed Book 2 then you should transfer all the information on your original Character Sheet to the one given here. You will carry five shuriken again, your flash powder will be replaced if you used it, and your Endurance and Inner Force will have been restored after your rest at the Temple of the Rock. You also continue Book 3 with any special items you may have picked up in your journey to the Island of Tranquil Dreams, and do not forget to transfer all your Punch, Kick, etc, Modifiers to your new Character Sheet.

You have also gained much experience in the Way of the Tiger in your previous adventures. Because of this you have improved your martial art skills through constant use. Add +1 to any two of your Punch, Kick, and/or Throw Modifiers. For instance, you may choose a +1 to Kick and a +1 to Throw. Should you fail in your mission and wish to try again from the start of this book, you may reconsider which Modifiers you raise.

When you are ready to begin the adventure, turn to **1**.

You walk beside the Grandmaster of the Dawn across the hot red sands to the Temple of the Rock. The tiger heads on the great golden doors stare balefully as you mount the marble steps; their eyes, priceless fire opals, glower redly. The Grandmaster says, 'The temple is to lose its most powerful protector.' You start and lay your hand upon his, but he continues, 'Not I, not I, it is you, Avenger, who must leave us once more.' You are about to protest but you cannot shirk your destiny so you wait to hear the Grandmaster's revelations. The temple doors swing open before you, the young acolytes bow and you proceed into the cool half-light of the temple. As you pass between the tigers' heads the birthmark on your thigh tingles suddenly and you instinctively cover the crown-shaped mark with your palm.

The Grandmaster speaks. 'The first-born of your family for four generations have carried the mark of the missionary king. Your father was called Loremaster Szeged and he was Overlord of a great city in the Manmarch, Irsmuncast, the last stronghold of men before the Rift, which men call the Bowels of Orb. He was one of the wise synod, the Loremasters of Serakub, but he became a missionary carrying the word of Kwon the Redeemer into the Manmarch.

'He became the High Priest at the Temple to Kwon in Irsmuncast and in time through his wisdom and fair-mindedness he became King. He ruled benignly and well and was beloved of all, save the reverencers of Nemesis, the Supreme Principle of Evil, and the riff-raff of thieves and cut-throats that gather in any great city. But when the monks of the Scarlet Mantis wished to build a temple to Vile beside the Temple of Avatar the One your father opposed this. He was a great martial arts warrior but he met his match and died at the hands of Yaemon, Grandmaster of Flame.

'So I named you aptly, Avenger, for you have already avenged your father's death, but now you must take back the crown which is rightfully yours. A cruel Usurper was set on the throne by Yaemon's wicked deed, and since that day he has twisted the city into a dark mirror of its former self. Now it is a bastion of evil and its citizens, your people, live in fear.

You must cast down the Usurper and rule in his place.' The Grandmaster hands you your father's seal which bears the mark of a hippogriff on a chequered background.

Turn to **14**.

2

You begin to tell Doré le Jeune your story. He is a sympathetic listener and you confide in him fully. He wishes you luck in your bid to topple the Usurper and he invites you to mount up before him, which you gladly do. After a while he turns the charger away from the Rift in the direction of Irsmuncast. He soon guides the conversation to the topic of the god, Kwon the Redeemer. It becomes obvious to you that he is passionately interested in theology and, on one occasion, as you twist your head to look at him, you catch a look of pure zeal in his eyes that is frightening in its intensity.

At length he says, 'But it is not enough to worship Kwon the Redeemer, who would tolerate a follower of the Chaos god, Béatan the Free, as easily as a true follower of Eo, the Prince of Peace and Weal.'

The young man's wordy preaching is becoming a trifle oppressive. Do you reply that Kwon stands for Law as well as Good and you see it as your duty to convert others to this faith (turn to **155**) or chide the young man gently saying that a free spirit is freer to do good (turn to **169**)?

3

Your pace never slackens for ten miles, by which time the Legion of the Sword of Doom has lost your trail. You pause to examine Honoric's leather pouch. It contains a Potion of Healing in a crystal bottle. You can drink it at any time when you are not in combat to restore up to 10 points of lost Endurance. Note it on your Character Sheet and turn to **13**.

4

It seems that the Rift affords the only remaining chance to rid yourself of the Golem's pursuit. You must lure the Golem to the Rift and then try to send it over the edge of the chasm to depths unknown. Turn to **352**.

You are running lightly under the rising sun of a new day when a figure, sitting cross-legged at the side of the path, comes into view ahead. As you draw closer you see that his eyes are closed in silent meditation. A long spear with a curved blade, a naginata, lies at his side. He is covered in a large scarlet robe, so that his hands are hidden. As you approach he opens his eyes and looks up at you with a smile of greeting. His face is almost square, his neck thick with muscle. A pair of green eyes seem to sparkle with malicious humour. He stands up and nods at you. Then he slings off his robe, revealing the bright red loose jacket and trousers of a Monk of the Scarlet Mantis, the followers of Vile. You step back, readying yourself for combat, but the monk just smiles. A leather belt, holding several daggers, runs across his chest. An unusually shaped short bow hangs at his back and a quiver of ten brightly feathered arrows hangs at his side. He speaks, a rasping, gravelly sound.

'Welcome Avenger. We of the Scarlet Mantis have heard you were abroad on the Manmarch again. I had hoped you would come this way. You have incurred the wrath of some very powerful people and, eh, certain divine beings. It is time that the death of our Grandmaster, Yaemon, was avenged and that the wrongs you have perpetrated against the great god Vile, Insuperable Master of Unarmed Combat and Speaker of Unholy Words, are righted. This requires, of course, your death. So, I, Aiguchi the Weaponmaster, known to some as the Dagger, will finish you. However, we shall not fall to blows here and now, like common peasants. Besides, you could escape me too easily. No, we shall fight a duel! Have you heard off the Ring of Vasch-Ro, ninja? No? It lies just beyond the next rise and it is an arena, maintained by Legionaries of the Sword of Doom, where duels of honour are fought.'

He pauses for a moment, and then in ringing tones he says, 'Avenger, I challenge you, and I invoke the power of Fate in the Ring of Vasch-Ro.' A moment's silence seems to fall all around as if he had indeed invoked some kind of power. 'I shall prove to you, in the Ring, ninja, how Kwon is

as nothing in the face of the teachings of Vile.'

Will you accept the challenge of Aiguchi (turn to **70**) or decide that you cannot afford to take unnecessary risks and continue on your way (turn to **25**)?

6

Back in the street once more you consider where to go next. If you have already visited the three largest inns tonight or do not wish to visit another, you return to the Temple to Kwon (turn to **417**). If not, you can visit the Cleansing Flame (turn to **105**), the Hostel from the Edge (turn to **78**) or the River of Beasts (turn to **62**), each only if you have not done so already.

7

You wend your way through the cemetery to the tomb of Lord Kalmon. You pass through the ornately-carved portals of the entrance into the darkness below. You draw out a torch and light it. It splutters into flame, filling the tomb with a flickering red glow, illuminating the single sarcophagus in the centre of the ancient chamber.

You walk to the wall beyond the sarcophagus and pull at the wrought iron torch bracket. There is a low rumble and a section of the wall slides open. The mechanism is well-oiled and the wall is free of dust. This entrance has been used recently – perhaps even regularly. Beyond the opening a flight of rough-hewn steps leads downwards into darkness. You come out into a corridor, cold flagstones lining the floor. As you walk around, the light from your torch, like a moving globe of luminescence, reveals painted murals on the walls. They show scenes of battle between men and many different types of creatures: Orcs, Dark Elves, Ogres and other hideous monsters. You recognise the coat of arms of your family on many of the human warriors.

After a while you come to the end of the corridor, an archway leading to blackness beyond. If you carry a Jade Lotus flower given to you by Golspiel, turn to **16**. Otherwise, turn to **28**.

8

You are taken to the Palace and left to languish in a prison cell until morning. It is the work of only a few minutes to loosen your bonds, and you trick the guard into coming close to the bars and then reach through them, grabbing his hair and cracking his head on the iron so that he falls unconscious. His key ring is within reach, and you free yourself from the cell and manage to cross the Palace's garden wall just before dawn. You hide on the roof of a nearby house during the day but at dusk you return to the Green and take the other main street eastwards in search of the Temple to Kwon. Turn to **269**.

9

Back at the Temple to Kwon, you tell the High Grandmaster that you will make your attempt on the Usurper's life tomorrow, when he will be sitting in judgement on more wrongly-accused innocents in the Throne Room. The High Grandmaster tells you that the dungeon the soothsayer spoke of leads directly into the Throne Room and you agree that it will provide an ideal route of attack against the unsuspecting Usurper. The Grandmaster cautions you that men tell awful tales of horrors that lurk below the Palace, but that he knows of a secret way into the dungeons. If you search out the tomb of the long-dead Lord Kalmon in the cemetery and pull down on the torch bracket that lights his epitaph, a doorway will open. He also reminds you of the soothsayer's words: that once within the dungeons, the tomb of Telmain III holds an item that will aid you. It seems the mausoleum keeps a circlet which holds a potent magic against the Usurper.

You tell the High Grandmaster that the signal for the monks to attack will be the lowering of the Usurper's flag on the Palace. When all of your preparations are complete you retire to meditate and then sleep. In the morning you walk, alone, towards the cemetery, dwelling on the High Grandmaster's last words to you. 'Farewell and remember, Avenger, many before have tried to kill the Usurper and failed. May Kwon guide you.' Turn to **7**.

You wait for Aiguchi to swing the spear at you in an arc, then you dart inside the reach of the blade and spin to face the shaft, driving your hand down in a Tiger's Paw chop, giving a cry as you call on your Inner Force. Deduct 1 from your Inner Force score. Treat the weapon's Defence as 6. If you succeed, turn to **177**. If you fail, turn to **126**.

You suggest to Doré le Jeune that you move away from the Bowels of Orb. If you decide to trust him and tell him who you are and what your business in Irsmuncast is, turn to **2**. If you prefer to keep your own confidence, turn to **47**.

You whip a needle to your mouth and send it flying towards him. He rears back in surprise and the needle slaps into his arm. He stares at it for a moment and then utters a low moan, rising to a shrieking crescendo as the poison courses through his body. He staggers back, writhing, but then incredibly begins to recover, his screams changing to heavy pants as he gulps in the air. He looks at you, glaring wildly. 'You will pay for that,' he whispers. You may note that he has lost 4 from his Endurance of 14. Suddenly he snarls. The lips draw back over his teeth and there is a wet tearing sound as, horribly, his jaw elongates, splitting out of his skull. His teeth grow in front of your very eyes, the canines shooting forwards. Fur begins to sprout all over him and his arms and legs crack and shudder, the bones growing, his hands and feet lengthening into taloned paws. His eyes burn with feral ferocity, the pupils changing into cat-like slits, glowing redly. You stand shocked into immobility for a moment as a man becomes a wolf before you. Then the Werewolf throws back his head and howls a long ululating call, a terrible sound that echoes around the chamber, filling your soul with dread. He drops to all fours and leaps towards you, snarling ferociously. At this you are galvanised into action, virtually a reflex for you now. If you have the skill of Acrobatics and wish to leap above his charge, turn to **341**. If you have a

Silver Shuriken or Enchanted Shuriken and wish to throw it, turn to **200**. Otherwise will you use an Iron Fist punch (turn to **67**), a Forked Lightning kick (turn to **219**) or the Teeth of the Tiger (turn to **364**)?

13

Knowing word that you are in the Manmarch will be spreading far and wide by now, you decide to turn south-east along the edge of the Barrow Swales, hoping to keep the secret of your destination cloaked in mystery. You are traveling through a gentle landscape, rolling meadows with small hamlets nestling in the valleys. You would expect to hear the summer sounds of wildlife all around you, but it is almost as if winter had come early and the birds had flown to warmer climes south of the Mountains of Horn. At mid-day you come across a badger cowering amongst the rot of last year's leaves for no apparent reason. Grim with foreboding you quicken your pace, relentlessly striding out the miles. Your new course takes you within sight of the domes and spires of a great city. It is the Spires of Foreshadowing, larger even than Doomover, and is the largest city in the Manmarch. It lies within a sea of rippling corn on the banks of the Greenblood. You decide to avoid the distractions of the city and turn again into the hills.

Exhausted after the rigours of the day, you stop at evening in the Barrow Swales and settle down to sleep. The stillness around you is eerie and you have not seen even a rabbit all day; normally they would be bounding out of your path in their scores, for their burrows are all around and before dusk they should be grazing. Your sleep is troubled by a low moaning somewhere in your dreams – it is you, crying at the news of your parents' death long ago. Then the vision of a figure more terrible than anything from your worst nightmares forms in your mind's eye. At first all you can see is a shadow, its edges flickering with dark fire, then a hawk-faced being a hundred feet tall takes shape. Its skin is silver, its eyes pools of blackness. The black fire which covers its sable robes is tinged with violet. It is Nemesis, Lord of the Cleansing Fire – Supreme Principle of Evil, the most powerful of the evil gods and the might of his thought is bent towards you. Even now a monster with supernatural powers responds to his call. Turn to **40**.

14

'But I know nothing of ruling men', you protest. 'Nevertheless,' says the Grandmaster, 'you have proven yourself to be powerful even amongst the most powerful on Orb and it is your destiny. If anyone can right the wrongs inflicted by the Usurper upon the poor people of Irsmuncast it is you. Kwon will guide you and I will teach you what I can, not of statecraft, your own wisdom must guide you there, but of the Way of the Tiger. You may learn another of the skills which you have not yet learnt, or I can teach you one of the two skills now known only to me: Shin-Ren, the Training of the Heart, or the martial skills of Yubi-Jutsu, Nerve-Striking. Shin-Ren, the Training of the Heart, will allow you to hone your instincts so that you may 'read' people like an open book. You will learn the language that the body talks, understanding what a person is thinking by observing their mannerisms and the way they breathe, the roving of their eyes and their stance. You will be able to understand a complicated situation at a glance and act appropriately, see any opening and take any chance that appears. In addition, you will be able to endure heat, cold, wind, rain, hunger, thirst and pain, control all of your feelings even more than before. Yubi-Jutsu is the most deadly skill known to the monks of Kwon bar Kopo-Jutsu, Bone-Breaking. Yubi-Jutsu is the martial skill of Nerve-Striking. You will learn how to maim and kill with even quite light blows to vital nerve centres, a technique especially useful when beset by many adversaries at once, or against a formidable human foe.'

If you ask to learn Shin-Ren, turn to **26**.
If you ask to learn Yubi-Jutsu, turn to **39**.
If you wish to learn another skill of the Way of the Tiger,
    turn to **50**.

The journey is uneventful and you spend most of your time meditating and exercising, preparing yourself for the trials you know will soon be upon you. The spice trader takes you across the sea to the southern edge of the Island of Plenty. At night you use a rowboat to slip to the forested shore. The ship then continues on to the port of Iga, whilst you travel to the Palace of the Shogun to pay your respects. You plan afterward to continue east to the port of Lemné and take ship from there to the mainland of Orb and the Manmarch. As you travel northwards through the rich and bountiful fields, you reflect on how peaceful the land has become since your last visit. The Shogun of the Island of Plenty, Kiyamo, has obviously been hard at work since you last stayed with him.

A few days later you reach the Palace of the Shogun which lies in a shallow valley between two peaks. Kiyamo is an old friend and he may be of service to you in your quest. You tell the gate guards, two samurai warriors in red lacquered armour, that you are Avenger from the Island of Tranquil Dreams and that you wish to see the Shogun. Presently you are led into a long chamber of polished wood. Armed samurai line the walls. Kiyamo sits cross-legged in front of a low table, while beside him stands Onikaba, his chief adviser.

If you have played Book 2, *ASSASSIN!*, and you helped Kiyamo by stealing into the camp of the evil Daimyo, Jikkyu, and killing him, turn to **271**. If not, turn to **304**.

You step through the archway and your torch illuminates a natural cavern and another carved archway in the wall opposite you. Suddenly there is a slight sound and a lantern flares up near the opposite archway, startling you. A man is standing beside it. He is naked save for a loincloth, and unarmed. He is slim and wiry, with dark eyes that seem to glitter with a sinister lustre in the low light. You cannot help noticing that he is unusually hirsute. You regard each other in silence for a moment. Then he takes a slow step towards you and then another, with great deliberation, his eyes never leaving yours. As he draws a little closer you can see the flickering flame of your torch reflected in his eyes and it seems as if you are looking directly into the fires of his soul.

He stops some fifteen feet away from you and sinks into a half crouch, his elbows tucked in at the waist, staring at you with a burning intensity as if he yearned for something only you could give him. He snarls, his teeth large and sharp, glinting in the torchlight. Then he speaks slowly, his voice deep and mellow, almost a purr. 'Greetings. You must be the rightful Overlord of Irsmuncast. Golspiel has told me all about you.'

He stands still as stone, only the jaws moving. Make a Fate roll. If Fate smiles on you, turn to **37**. If not, turn to **242**.

17

Since you have not chosen to learn one of the skills known only to the Grandmaster of the Dawn, he, disappointed, gives you over to the tutelage of the other Grandmasters. They teach you your new skill painstakingly over a period of several weeks, during which you do little else but practise, praying to Kwon that he may grant you mastery of the new skill. At length you have mastered it. Note your new skill on your Character Sheet. Turn to **291**.

18

Glaivas runs to you as your battered body, until now motionless, slumps when your mind takes up its natural abode once more. He lays you gently on the soft carpet of pine needles and, asking what happened, begins to use his healing arts. You regain 6 points of lost Endurance but the pain mars your sleep. In the morning you insist that you are well enough to continue and set off soon after sunrise. Turn to **414**.

19

If you have a Yellow China Flower turn to **49**. If not you wend your way between the debauched-looking customers to the low chess table and pretend to study a chess problem for a while. You have not been there long and conversation has started again, when a young man in a grey doublet and hose sits opposite you, pours two glasses of wine and offers to give you a game. Seeing this is an ideal opportunity to get to know someone who is not a peasant, you agree readily. He gives you white but you nevertheless play an uncharacteristically defensive pawn formation. 'The shieldmaiden's reserve,' comments your opponent. 'You are not, by any chance, a reverencer of Dama?' You shake your head innocently, and a woman with plucked eyebrows and eye kohl on an adjoining chaise-longue laughs and says, 'Thank the Dark-Lord for that! Their prowess with the sword is already too much without their beating us at the game of chess as well.' Some of the soldiers howl at her but she waves her black lace fan at them, 'Why then, can you not stop them drilling and parading as if it were they who ruled the city?' This provokes a hostile outcry but the woman ignores it and attempts to hide herself in your game. Your opponent introduces himself as Radziwil and the woman is Elektra. They talk quietly for a time, not excluding you, of the bad feeling that exists for the Usurper within the city. At length Radziwil turns to you and says, 'What do you think? Irsmuncast could do with a new ruler.' Will you agree quietly but heartily and say that you know of a possible candidate (turn to **84**) or say that Irsmuncast seems a fair and fine city (turn to **98**)?

20

Your hand a blur of movement, you send a shuriken spinning towards him. He starts in surprise and your aim is true. The shuriken embeds itself in his shoulder, and he utters a shrill scream of pain. Roll one die and note that he has lost this amount from his Endurance of 14. Suddenly he snarls. The lips draw back over his teeth and there is a wet tearing sound as, horribly, his jaw elongates, splitting out of his skull. His teeth grow in front of your very eyes, the canines shooting forwards. Fur begins to sprout all over him and his arms and legs crack and shudder, the bones growing, his hands and feet lengthening into taloned paws. His eyes burn with feral ferocity, the pupils changing into cat-like slits, glowing redly. You stand shocked into immobility for a moment as a man becomes a wolf before you. Then the Werewolf throws back his head and howls a long ululating call, a terrible sound that echoes around the chamber, filling your soul with dread. He drops to all fours and leaps towards you, snarling ferociously. At this you are galvanised into action, virtually a reflex for you now. If you have the skill of Acrobatics and wish to leap above his charge, turn to **341**. If you have a Silver Shuriken or Enchanted Shuriken and wish to throw it, turn to **200**. Otherwise will you use an Iron Fist punch (turn to **67**), a Forked Lightning kick (turn to **219**) or the Teeth of the Tiger (turn to **364**)?

21

At last you sight the estuary of the river Greybones and the ship glides past the harbour of Ilvontor and on up the winding reaches towards the great city of Tor. There the sailors moor on the grain wharf and you instruct them to trade their cargo and buy another before they set sail for the Island of Plenty, pretending that they are merchantmen. Tor is a huge city of half a million souls, but you know that your friend Glaivas the Ranger lives on Temple Street. You make your way there passing as you do so a church to Vasch-Ro, the god of mortal combat and another to Moraine, the god of Empire. Glaivas himself reveres the All-Mother, but his town house is beyond the Temple to Avatar the One. If you have the skill of Shin-Ren, turn to **407**. If not, turn to **393**.

22

You run at Aiguchi and leap into the air in a drop kick, trying to lock your feet around his head, but he is too quick. He jumps back and slashes at your legs with his naginata, opening a nasty wound in your left calf. Lose 4 Endurance. If you are still alive, you realise you will be unable to get close enough to Aiguchi to throw him because of the extra reach he has with the naginata. As you stand up, he rushes at you, the naginata above his head, pointing down at you. You jump aside and you may now attack again. Will you use the Tiger's Paw chop (turn to **38**), the Leaping Tiger kick (turn to **56**) or wait for a suitable moment and, using Inner Force, attempt to snap his naginata (turn to **10**)?

23

You turn away from the dangers of the Rift but your legs will take you no further. You are forced to give battle once again, in the hope that this time you can truly destroy it, but you no longer have the strength to defeat the powerful monster. Its knobbled fists close on your throat and the life is choked out of you.

24

You dive after the tramp and grab his cloak as if to throttle him, but the Usurper's soldiers are rushing in on you from all sides of the cobbled yard. You leave the tramp, but a Yellow China Flower comes away in your hand from under his robe. Note that you have this on your Character Sheet. You somersault over the heads of the soldiers and out through the archway once more, then manage to elude them in the dark streets and find yourself back at the Green. You decide this time to take the street leading east (turn to **269**).

25

The eyes of the worshipper of Vile widen in surprise as you refuse his challenge, but then he smiles gleefully. 'So be it, ninja. May your journey be fruitful,' he says wryly. Then he walks past you and heads off towards Doomover. You are thinking about his strangely unaggressive behaviour when a strange chill takes hold and a wave of nausea washes over you for a second. You have been cursed by Fate because you refused the challenge of the Ring of Vasch-Ro and she has turned her back on you. You will fail the next three Fate Rolls. Note this down on your Character Sheet. Dejectedly you press on towards Irsmuncast nigh Edge. Turn to **416**.

26

The Grandmaster of the Dawn says, 'A good choice, Avenger. I will teach you all I know of Shin-Ren, the Training of the Heart.' You spend many weeks in his company, learning the secret knowledge. He has iron control of his emotions, can walk barefoot over glowing coals and, at the end, you both fast for twenty days without feeling hunger. You had never suspected how little details of the way you hold your head or when you blink gave so much away about your heart, but now the language of the body is known to you and you can read people's hearts at a glance. It pleases you to note that most of those who live on the Island of Tranquil Dreams are honest and open, hiding nothing. Note that you are an adept in the skill of Shin-Ren on your Character Sheet and turn to **291**.

27

At last Aiguchi lies dead at your feet. You kneel down beside him and search his body. Amongst his weapons you find two bottles. One is filled with a green liquid and is a Potion of Healing. You may drink it at any time and gain up to 10 points of lost Endurance. The other is filled with a blue liquid and is labelled 'Waters of Protection from Ethereal Flame'. Note these on your Character Sheet. Shouldering Aiguchi's body, you take it with you through the Victor's Gate. Beyond the Gate is a small hut. As you approach it, Maak emerges hurriedly, but pulls up with a look of disappointment on his face as he sees who is dead and who still lives. 'I see you triumphed once again, ninja,' he says angrily. 'By the laws of the Ring you are now free to go. But once you have left this place you will be fair game for your enemies once more. And you have many enemies, ninja.' With that he turns on his heel and walks into the hut. You leave the body of Aiguchi outside the hut and run on, heading for Irsmuncast. Turn to **416**.

28

You step through the archway and your torch illuminates a natural cavern, the flames creating a thousand flickering shadows around its walls. Straight ahead lies another archway and you cross the cavern floor, eyes and ears alert for anything unexpected, but everything is quiet. Entering the archway you continue on. After a few yards a foul odour

reaches your nostrils from up ahead, and strange snarling sounds echo down the tunnel. Rounding a bend you can see distant torchlight. Quickly you douse your torch and edge your way silently towards the source of light. As you do so, the sound and smell grow stronger. Soon you are hidden in the shadows of the tunnel, looking into a large square room carved out of the rock. In its centre stands a large fire, smoke billowing up to be lost in the darkness above. Around it are arranged two long oak tables, strewn with all kinds of food and drink, mostly meat, half raw and half eaten. At the tables sit three bulky beasts dressed in greasy leather armour, with large wooden clubs at their side. They are gross and misshapen, their skin a greyish-green colour, warty and mottled. Their fat faces have wide-splayed nostrils and rotting teeth. Their huge beards are matted with filth. You recognise them as Cave Trolls.

What interests you most is the blackened and stained livery they are wearing, for it is the stag with the spiral-horned antlers, the symbol of the Usurper. It seems these Cave Trolls are in his service, kept out of harm's way down here but ready to be called upon if necessary. They are drinking heavily and arguing amongst themselves, their growling voices animal-like, barely discernible. Beyond them you can see another archway where the corridor continues. You can see no other exit. You must try to get through. If you have the skill of Climbing you may try to climb upwards into the shadows and make your way around the cavern to the exit (turn to **94**). Otherwise, or if you do not wish to climb, you may sprint straight out to the fire and throw your flash powder onto it, and then sprint for the exit (turn to **102**).

You lose your grip and plunge down the precipice to your death. The Golem pounds your dead body to a pulp with its hammer fists.

The devils close in and together they are too strong for you. Suddenly there is a grating noise of granite on marble as the statue of the goddess Dama comes to life. You shelter behind it as her sword, glowing silver, flashes through the air. The statue may triumph, but Scourge has moved behind it to attack you. Once again you decide to use kicks against him as he is too tall for punches to really affect him.

SCOURGE THE CENTAUR DEVIL
Defence against Leaping Tiger kick: 7
Defence against Kwon's Flail: 5
Damage: 2 Dice + 2
Endurance: 22

Note that any injuries you previously inflicted on Scourge still apply. Your blows affect Scourge as if he were a normal beast, while he is not in hell, but Inner Force does not affect him. The Saint's Locket and the Ruby Circlet will protect you against Scourge as they did against Astaroth, as the Centaur Devil rears and smashes down his iron hooves to stave in your skull. Your Defence as you try to leap aside is 7, or 8 if you have the skill of Acrobatics. If Scourge is still attacking, you must kick him again.

If you win, Scourge disappears, banished to the spirit plane, and Astaroth alone of the devils remains. The statue returns to its pedestal and becomes stone again. You must fight Astaroth once more, and you decide to use the Iron Fist punch against him as he is much weakened by the statue's attentions and magical blade.

ASTAROTH
Defence against Iron Fist punch: 8
Damage: 3 Dice
Endurance: 2

Special conditions no longer apply when striking him. When defending yourself, the Saint's Locket and the Ruby Circlet protect as before. If you win, turn to **189**. If Astaroth fights on, you try to avoid his champing jaws, and your Defence is 8. If you survive you punch again.

31
Your Training of the Heart tells you much about this stranger. You can trust him. He is of open character and what he tells you is true. He has dedicated his life to fighting evil and is no more nor less insane than you. He shows no fear of you but this is not arrogance nor the inexperience of youth. The signs are that he would be a powerful friend or a worthy adversary. Turn to **11**.

32
As you run on there is a heavy blow on your back and you are thrown onto your face in the corn. Before you realise what has happened, Glaivas has pulled the spear out and you are up and running once more. There is no time to heal or bind the wound, which is bleeding heavily. Lose 6 Endurance. However, if you are still alive, your pursuers are soon flagging and you draw away. Turn to **264**.

33
From the general conversation, you gather that the clientele of the Hostel from the Edge may have private grudges

against the Usurper, but they do not voice them. Some of the men whisper amongst themselves, but stop whenever the tramp staggers past. You overhear some Orcs talking with relish of the breaking on the wheel of two innocent scapegoats above the gates to the park, in full view of the Temple to Kwon. Hearing this, you decide to slip out of the inn, back to the Green and then turn east again to find the temple. Turn to **269**.

34

You follow the dirty white stones through the trees, ears and eyes straining, your senses tingling, but you find nothing unusual as you creep stealthily through the woods, almost without trace. After a while the trees thin out and you come to the edge of the wood. Gently rolling ground carpeted in long grass leads to a disorganised pile of chalky rocks and boulders, lining the rim of Hunter's Quarry. As stealthily as possible, you continue following the stones, giving the Quarry a wide berth. Suddenly the air is filled with a loud high-pitched whine. You spin to see Aiguchi silhouetted against the Quarry stones. You realise he is using Humming Bulb arrows, fluted to whistle and whine in the air. Do you have the skill of Arrow Cutting? If you do, turn to **63**. If you do not, turn to **92**.

35

On the next day your progress becomes slower as you wind your way over a series of forested gullies, telling Glaivas of your dreams as you go. He says that he is unable to reach the spirit planes, but he gives you a piece of mandrake root, like a little misshapen man, and says that if you wish to reach the spirit plane, eating the root will help to prepare your mind for the journey. As night approaches it begins to rain and the moisture soaks slowly through the trees. Turn to **419**.

36

You strike too late and once again find yourself thrown to the ground. But there is an agonizing pain in your neck as the leopard tears at your jugular vein. Blood gushes, then the leopard rolls over, Glaivas' sword in its back. You have lost 9 Endurance, but if you still live then Glaivas speaks a word of healing which staunches the gushing hot blood. He seems saddened by the death of the leopard, almost as if it were a bad omen, but he tells you where to watch for them lurking in the trees as you walk on.

Turn to **44**.

37

The man reaches up, brushing at his lips as if in anticipation of a fine meal, and you see that the palms of his hands are covered in hair.

Will you wait to see what he does next (turn to **242**) or will you attack him, either by using Poison Needles against him, if you have that skill (turn to **12**), hurling a shuriken at him (turn to **20**) or, if you have one, hurling a silver shuriken or enchanted shuriken at him (turn to **45**)?

38

You dodge in, past a thrust of Aiguchi's naginata, and chop at his neck.

AIGUCHI THE WEAPONMASTER
Defence against Tiger's Paw chop: 6
Endurance: 15
Damage: 2 Dice

If you have reduced him to 4 or less Endurance, turn to **289**. If not, he jumps back and, using a reverse strike, sends the iron shod end of his naginata hurtling at your head. Your Defence is 7 as you try to duck. If he hits you, the butt of the spear cracks into your skull sending you staggering back.

If you are still alive, you can use the Tiger's Paw chop again (return to the top of this paragraph), attack with the Leaping Tiger kick (turn to **56**) or the Teeth of the Tiger throw (turn to **22**), or you can wait for a suitable moment and, using Inner Force, attempt to snap Aiguchi's naginata (turn to **10**).

39

The Grandmaster of the Dawn is pleased that you have chosen to learn one of the skills known only to him. You spend many weeks learning the anatomy of man, the unprotected points where the nerves meet and where an accurate blow can stun or even kill. After much practice, the Grandmaster tells you that your prowess outshines even his own. Note that you are an adept at the skill of Yubi-Jutsu on your Character Sheet and turn to **291**.

40

For some reason you find yourself dreaming of a great city which you have never visited but is clear in every detail in your dream. It is as if you are hovering above it on a cloudless night. The wide avenues are lined with magical lamps in which orange flames flicker, casting a dull brown glow over the canopy of the night sky. It is a city of great domes and spires and at its centre one great towered dome larger than any building you have ever set eyes upon. You fly beyond it, like a night owl, to a magnificent spired palace, through jewelled gates and through huge rooms lined with velvet, halls with crystal chandeliers and wide marble staircases. A macabre sense of witless purpose grips you, forcing you onto the top of the central spire, the master bedroom. But your dream does not take you through the great doors of solid gold that bar entrance to the chamber, for you have already found the object of your quest. Arms akimbo beside the doors stands a towering figure, seven feet tall. It is naked but those parts which would determine its sex are missing, there is just a scar there. The face and head are a man's but do not appear to fit the neck. It is a Golem, the parts of many dead bodies stitched together and reanimated magically. The personal bodyguard of Dom the Prescient, ruler of the Spires of Foreshadowing. As you watch in your mind's eye, the unnatural monster opens its eyes and speaks in a cracked voice long disused, 'Avenger!' The Golem of Flesh takes a ponderous step towards the staircase. You wake sitting bolt upright in a cold sweat. Turn to **55**.

As you make your speech you can see some of the crowd becoming restless and looking questioningly from you to the Demagogue. It seems that they are not taking to you as their new leader. You try to rally them but the meeting becomes a shouting match and then there is a battering at the street door. The Usurper's soldiers have arrived to disperse the mob and it begins to break up. The Demagogue takes your hand, saying, 'They will not fight now,' and leads you out by the secret back entrance. You make your way away from the soldiers and you can only hope that the rabble will rise up when you have killed the Usurper. If you wish to approach another faction with whom you have not yet spoken, will it be the priesthood at the Temple to Time (turn to **394**), the Swordswomen of Dama, Shieldmaiden of the Gods (turn to **296**) or the merchants in their emporia (turn to **184**)? If you feel you have the support you need you make your final preparations to assassinate the Usurper (turn to **9**).

You just manage to regain your footing and climb on up the difficult north-west face of the peak, but to your dismay the monster follows. At last you hear the sound of a rockfall below and look down to see the monster tumbling and bouncing a thousand feet down an almost sheer face. At last the threat is lifted and you begin the descent, only to see the Golem clambering up towards you once more. There is only one narrow route if you wish to climb on (turn to **85**). If not, you may use the time gained by the Golem's fall to climb sideways and then down the north-east face (turn to **74**).

'I am Doré le Jeune, of the order of the Paladin Knights of Dragonhold and I journey to these infested regions for a tenday each year and wait for the Orcs to boil out of the Rift and attack me.' 'What then?' you ask. 'Why, then I smite them until they will trouble good men no more!' 'But what if Dark Elves attack you with sorcery?' The young man does not reply, but merely strokes his sword and smiles. You find it difficult to decide whether he is sensible or far gone in madness. If you have the skill of Shin-Ren, turn to **31**. If not turn to **11**.

44

Glaivas leads you on through the silent forest. The trees crowd in and you are walking uphill through a deep green gloom of straight pine trees. At last the Ranger brings you out to a leaf-littered clearing where you stop to rest. There are signs that some man-like being has lived in the clearing. You point them out and Glaivas says, 'The Forest-Sprites, they are mischief makers and sometimes worse, but I had hoped they might help us. They are in my debt.' 'I haven't seen any sign of them before,' you say and Glaivas replies, 'They are avoiding us, but take care of your belongings.'

As the gloom deepens the sense of dread that invaded your sleep yesternight descends again. When it is your turn to sleep your slumber is fitful and the dreams return to haunt you. You see huge threatening figures; one, hawk-faced, is more than a hundred feet tall. It is standing in Dis, the Iron-city of the Underworld. Before it something is being created in a gigantic black bubbling cauldron. You see a loathsome winged Fiend, like a son of Nil, shimmering in the steam. Then the dream changes, a great white leopard stalks towards you, and then you realise that it is not a leopard, but the blue-eyed Spirit Tiger that serves your god Kwon the Redeemer. She seems to be saying that when the malice of the gods of evil bears black fruit you must seek her on the spirit planes, where you wandered with the Grandmaster of the Dawn. When you awake Glaivas is preparing a breakfast of nuts and roots and as soon as you have eaten you set off again. Turn to **35**.

45

Your hand a blur of movement, you send the Shuriken spinning towards him. He starts in surprise and your aim is true. The Shuriken embeds itself in his shoulder. He staggers in pain but then begins to shriek in agony, clawing at the Shuriken as if it were burning into him. Desperately he rips it out and throws it aside, as if it were damaging even to his hand, and it is lost somewhere amid the stones. Cross it off your Character Sheet and note that he has lost 7 from his Endurance of 14.

Suddenly he snarls. The lips draw back over his teeth and there is a wet tearing sound as, horribly, his jaw elongates, splitting out of his skull. His teeth grow in front of your very eyes, the canines shooting forwards. Fur begins to sprout all over him and his arms and legs crack and shudder, the bones growing, his hands and feet lengthening into taloned paws. His eyes burn with feral ferocity, the pupils changing into cat-like slits, glowing redly. You stand shocked into immobility for a moment as a man becomes a wolf before you. Then the Werewolf throws back his head and howls a long ululating call, a terrible sound that echoes around the chamber, filling your soul with dread. He drops to all fours and leaps towards you, snarling ferociously. At this you are galvanised into action, virtually a reflex for you now. If you have the skill of Acrobatics and wish to leap above his charge, turn to **341**. Otherwise will you use an Iron Fist punch (turn to **67**), a Forked Lightning kick (turn to **219**) or the Teeth of the Tiger (turn to **364**)?

46

As Aiguchi lunges forward and sends the nunchaku whistling straight down at your head, you step to the side and grab his wrist. You try to grab his knee with your other hand and twist him over your hip.

AIGUCHI THE WEAPONMASTER
Defence against Whirlpool throw: 6
Endurance: 15
Damage: 1 Die + 1

If you have thrown Aiguchi successfully and have the skill of Yubi-Jutsu, turn to **65**. If you have thrown him but do not have the skill of Yubi-Jutsu, you slam him to the ground. You may use the Cobra Strike punch as he struggles to his feet, adding 2 to your Punch Modifier and damage for this attack only (turn to **303**). If you have failed to throw him, he twists away and flails at your ribs with the nunchaku. Your Defence is 6. If you are still alive you may punch (turn to **303**) or kick (turn to **89**) Aiguchi.

47

Tight-lipped you begin to walk away from the chasm. Doré le Jeune scrutinises you for a time before setting spur to his horse. Your last sight of him is as he reins in at the edge of the Rift and shouts a challenge to the Spawn of Evil to emerge from the dark to face him in battle. The great cry echoes from side to side of the enormous Rift and you make haste to lose yourself in the forest before turning north. Turn to **199**.

48

You move quickly through the wood, using your training in stealth to the full, and soon come out into a small clearing. The skeletal remains of a previous contestant lie at its centre, still clothed in rusted chain-mail, a shattered sword at its side. You notice a purse still attached to a rotted leather belt. Inside are several gold pieces, but money is not of importance right now. Senses straining for any signs of Aiguchi, you press on. Soon the trees begin to thin as you approach the edge of the Duelwood. Do you have the skill of Picking Locks, Detecting and Disarming Traps? If you do, turn to **157**. If not, turn to **182**.

49

You walk towards an empty table with a chess board on it, intending to pretend to study a chess problem, but as soon as you sit down a young man jumps up and denounces you as a traitor. You are surrounded by priests and priestesses of Nemesis and soldiers in the Usurper's army. Even for Avenger there is no escape.

50

If your chosen new skill is Immunity to Poisons, turn to **60**. If it is not, turn to **17**.

You have taken the mood of the crowd and they are carried on with you. They have accepted you as the rightful heir and their new leader. When you sit down they cheer you and then the Demagogue whips them into a frenzy of fervour. Suddenly there is a battering at the street door. The Usurper's soldiers have arrived to disperse the mob. Scuffles and fighting break out but the Demagogue takes your hand saying, 'We must make a plan'. He leads you out of the hall by the secret back door and you tell him that you will assassinate the Usurper and then pull down his flag on the Palace as a signal for the mob to attack the Palace, the barracks and the Temple to Nemesis. The Demagogue says that you may leave the rest to him. He presses a coin showing the head of your father and marked 'Coronation Day', into your hand. Note the Coronation Day Coin on your Character Sheet. If you wish to approach another faction with whom you have not yet spoken, will it be the priesthood at the Temple to Time (turn to **394**), the Swordswomen of Dama, Shieldmaiden of the Gods (turn to **296**) or the merchants in their emporia (turn to **184**)? If you feel you have the support you need, you make your final preparations to assassinate the Usurper (turn to **9**).

52

With a flash of insight you hit on a plan. You can lure the Golem to the Rift and then try to send it over the edge of the chasm to depths unknown. Turn to **352**.

53

The speed of the leopard takes you quite by surprise, far faster than a man. As it springs at your throat you lash out quickly with your fist. Its Defence against the Iron Fist punch is 7. If the leopard is too fast for you and you miss, turn to **36**. If not you jolt it backwards as Glaivas speaks a soothing word, then the leopard turns tail and is soon lost to sight, its spots merging with the dappled sunlight. As you journey on, Glaivas tells you where to watch out for leopards lurking in the trees. Turn to **44**.

54

Smothering any disgust you might feel at the ugliness of the noseless Halvorcs, you sit on the end of their bench. They are happy to talk to you about themselves and it seems they have a few scores to settle with the soldiers of the Usurper's army. You ask whether feeling runs high against the Usurper and they reply that it does. One of them asks you if there is a plot against him. You hesitate for a moment too long. A shadow falls over the bench and you spin round to see the tramp, quite sober, denouncing you as a traitor. The Halvorcs attack you and you deal death to two of them but you are caught in a powerful grip from behind. The Wolfen have joined the fray and at the end of a fierce battle one of them rips your throat out with a single swipe of his clawed hand.

55

Try as you might you cannot get back to sleep, a premonition of doom hanging heavily upon you. Wet with dew, you rise with the dawn mist and set off once more through the Barrow Swales. A strange sweet smell like honeysuckle wafts in the air, then a figure, arms outstretched towards you, sways out of the mist. It is the Golem of Flesh that guards the chambers of the ruler of the Spires. Once more it speaks your name, its voice cracking. Realising that it has been sent to kill you, you decide to give battle. Its movements are ponderous and heavy, its body seems to have been cobbled together from parts of many different men, some freckled, some yellow-skinned, some hirsute, and a sickly-sweet green fluid oozes over the joints. If you have the skill of Yubi-Jutsu, Nerve-Striking, and wish to use it, turn to **64**. If not, you decide against using a throw on the heavy monster. Will you attack it with the Forked Lightning kick (turn to **79**), the Leaping Tiger kick (turn to **88**), the Tiger's Paw chop (turn to **99**) or the Iron Fist punch (turn to **108**)?

56

Aiguchi slashes at you but you dive forward under the blade and roll to your feet, unleashing a Leaping Tiger as you come up, driving the ball of your foot at his head.

AIGUCHI THE WEAPONMASTER
Defence against Leaping Tiger kick: 7
Endurance: 15
Damage: 2 Dice

If you have reduced him to 4 or less Endurance, turn to **289**. If not, he twists aside twirling his naginata in a short arc, trying to cut at your chest. Your Defence is 7. If he hits you, the naginata slices across your chest.

If you are still alive, you can kick again (return to the top of this paragraph), attack with the Tiger's Paw chop (turn to **38**) or the Teeth of the Tiger throw (turn to **22**), or you can wait for a suitable moment and, using Inner Force, attempt to snap Aiguchi's naginata (turn to **10**).

57
At last you have slain the fell beast. You stand, breathing heavily for a moment. Did you lose any Endurance in your fight against the Werewolf? If you did, turn to **87**. If you did not, turn to **71**.

58
You forge straight down the Path of Fools. All is quiet in the Duelwood as you pad silently along the edge of the path. Rounding a bend, you come upon a grisly and disquieting sight. The skeletal remains of a former combatant are pinned to a tree by an old wooden spear. His clothing is rotting and his armour rusted. You continue on past the body – a grim reminder of what comes to pass in the Ring of Vasch-Ro – and are soon at a crossroads in the midst of the murky Duelwood. You pause, listening hard, but can detect no sign of Aiguchi.

Will you carry straight on towards the Victor's Gate (turn to **250**), go north (turn to **266**) or go south (turn to **82**)?

59
The crowd who have assembled to hear the Demagogue seem to be of two types of people. Some have the look of those who would live in a state of squalor no matter who

reigned over them, coarse-looking and unwashed. Many more, dressed in torn and patched clothing, have the look of those who have seen better days. There is a tense and angry mood in the hall. When the Demagogue stands he is mocked, but when he begins to speak it is as if the rabble has fallen under a spell. He is a superb orator and his words stir the crowd until they are chanting 'Death to the Usurper'. Even you feel the injustices of these people as if you too had suffered as he describes their plight.

'Who has usurped the land of your birth?'

'The Usurper!' shouts the crowd.

'Who has denied you the chance to raise children?'

'The Usurper!'

'Who has taken everything you ever had?'

'The Usurper!'

'And who will give these things back to you?'

There is a muffled shout of 'The Usurper,' then an uneasy silence settles over the crowd. 'No one,' says the Demagogue. 'You must take what is yours by birthright.' He continues until they are on their feet shouting again for the Usurper's death. 'And here is your leader, the child of the Loremaster, rightful Overlord, Avenger!'

You stand up to address the hysterical mob, a strange feeling of butterflies in your stomach. Will you tell them that you will restore their birthright, saying they have nothing to lose but their chains (turn to **51**) or say that the Usurper must be punished and that, with their help, you will be the new Overlord (turn to **41**)?

The Grandmaster of the Dawn seems disappointed that you have not chosen one of the two skills known only to him, but he tells you that you do not have time to acquire Immunity to Poisons. This requires the ingesting of ever-increasing doses of lethal poisons over many years. You must choose a different skill.

If you ask to learn Shin-Ren, turn to **26**.
If you ask to learn Yubi-Jutsu, turn to **39**.
If you wish to learn another skill of the Way of the Tiger, turn
   to **17**.

The speed of the leopard takes you quite by surprise, far faster than a man. You are bowled to the ground once more, but your block stops the leopard's fangs closing on your jugular vein and a word from Glaivas seem to quiet the animal, which trots away, soon lost to sight in the dappled sunlight. You thank Glaivas and journey on, whilst he tells you where to watch out for leopards lurking in the trees. Turn to **44**.

The inn called the River of Beasts is on a crooked line of flagstones called Izvestia Street. The sign outside it shows a sea serpent and grotesque snake-like horses and dogs frolicking in a frothing blue river. Inside you walk past two armed guards into a number of small rooms, each served by bars in which more than two hundred people are drinking and talking. The air is heavy with smoke and this is the first time that you have seen the common people of Irsmuncast appearing to enjoy themselves. You soon realise that you are being watched by the barman, so you sit quietly in a corner. A young serving boy gives you a drink by mistake and then gets cuffed round the head for his error by a hearty-looking red-bearded fellow. You offer him the stirrup cup but he motions you to keep it, so you drink slowly and keep your eyes open. It soon becomes obvious that the people speak openly here about their hatred of the Usurper and you ask Red-beard about the people's feelings. All that he tells you convinces you that, given a leader, someone to fight for, the rabble could rise up to throw off the yoke of tyranny. At least half of the able-bodied populace appear to have a burning grievance against the Usurper and in recent riots the soldiers, mainly Orcs, had to kill many of them to quell their revolutionary ardour. You say nothing of your own right to the throne but ask why they have no leaders. Red-beard tells you that they have a leader, the Demagogue, but that while he is a fine mob orator no-one would fight for him – he is hardly a dashing warrior. You ask him who he would like to ally himself with, the merchants, the priests of Time, or the Swordswomen of Dama, but he replies that the commoners need no allies. At length you decide to leave, much heartened by your talk with Red-beard and his friends. Turn to **6**.

63

You have barely enough time to register you are under attack, and the noise of the arrow screaming through the air towards you is distracting. Roll for a block as though you were deflecting a blow, treating your Defence as 8. If you succeed, turn to **113**. If you fail, turn to **103**.

64

Risking yourself in an attempt to stop the monster with a single blow, you jab your hand into the monster's solar plexus. Your fingers sink in leaving an unnatural hollow. However, the Golem does not depend on nerves to control its spasmodic movements but on the magic which animates it. Its heavy fist smashes down upon the top of your head. Lose 5 Endurance. If you are still alive, you attack again. Will you use the Forked Lightning kick (turn to **79**), the Leaping Tiger kick (turn to **88**), the Tiger's Paw chop (turn to **99**) or the Iron Fist punch (turn to **108**)?

65

You bring Aiguchi crashing onto his back. He lies stunned for a brief moment allowing you to choose your target and execute a precision nerve-strike. You drive two punches quick as lightning into nerve centres in his shoulder and neck. He dies instantly. You sit back, gulping great breaths of air, as you let your body relax. Turn to **27**.

66

At the third Death-Knell there is a great wailing from the Fiend which freezes you, paralyzed with terror. It reaches out to embrace you, but just before its arms close around you it begins to dissolve into black smoke. The smoke billows into a whirlpool then seems to disappear into its eye.

All is quiet but you feel exhilarated. You have cheated Nemesis, the Supreme Principle of Evil and banished his emissary back to the Iron-city of Dis, deep in the Underworld. You are able to move again and Glaivas, frozen in terror just as you were, begins to recover. He looks at you with renewed respect as you settle down to take what rest you can. Turn to **77**.

67

The creature jumps at you, jaws snapping. You side-step it and drive your fist at the side of its head.

WEREWOLF
Defence against Iron Fist punch: 6
Endurance: 14
Damage: 1 Die + 2

If you have killed it, turn to **57**. If it is still alive, it twists with incredible speed and tries to sink its teeth around your wrist. Your Defence is 7. If you are still alive, will you punch again (return to the top of this paragraph), kick (turn to **219**) or throw (turn to **364**) the beast?

68

When you tell the High Grandmaster at the Temple to Kwon that you have decided to enlist the support of the rabble he nods but says that it will not be easy. He introduces you to the man they call the Demagogue, who calls on you at the

Temple to Kwon. He is a tall but emaciated man, and his yellow robe flaps around legs no thicker than a sparrow's. His face is all nose, his lips narrow and twisted, but his eyes burn with a manic intensity. He seems nervous in the presence of the High Grandmaster, but he turns his unshifting gaze upon you and asks you to justify yourself. You tell him you would strive to rule as wisely as the Loremaster your father, and be fair to all. After long discussion, the Demagogue warns that you will need to impress the rabble greatly if you are to whip them up into a frenzy and unite them behind you but that he will work on them first. That evening he takes you to a great meeting hall behind the River of Beasts Inn where hundreds of malcontents are waiting for a speech. Turn to **59**.

69

As you look back to the hedge of thorns you are dismayed to see a concealed gateway opening in its side and fifty or more Halvorcs pouring out of it. As the blackhawk still circles above you, you run on, covering the ground more easily now that you are out of the corn. Glaivas suggests that you keep going. He is more worried at the prospect of other, more powerful, minions of Death learning that you are abroad, than by the Halvorcs, and he regrets that he has not brought his long bow. The Halvorcs cannot match your pace but any Orcs among them will be able to track you by smell. Glaivas tells you that the land between here and the City of the Runes of Doom is dotted with forbidding castles around a flat plain called the Slave Fields. You slip past a turreted keep and, at dusk, onto the Slave Fields. The slaves are staked out under canvas awnings next to the fields which they are harvesting. There are orcish guards with each group. Glaivas tells you that by order of the Fleshless King, only Orcs may be used as overseers as they have never been known to show humans the slightest compassion. Glaivas motions you to hide with him behind a tree and then puts a choice to you. He fears that the gods of evil may have found a way to let the Fleshless King know who you are. The blackhawk is gone, but vampire bats flit past. The choice is between running on, all night (turn to **83**), or trying to creep under one of the canvas awnings to hide (turn to **91**).

70

Aiguchi the Weaponmaster smiles chillingly and says, 'Follow me then.' He leads you over the crest of the hill. Below lies a low-roofed stone building in a cultivated field. Beyond it can be seen a small but thick wood. As you draw nearer, a group of men you recognise as soldiers from the Legion of the Sword of Doom step out of the house. However, they do not seem to be looking for trouble. One of them, a sharp quick man with brown eyes and curly brown hair says, 'Welcome once again, Aiguchi – do you require the services of the Ring?'

'Yes Maak, I do. Allow me to introduce my latest opponent,' and he indicates you. 'This is the ninja, Avenger, the one who slew Yaemon, Manse the Deathmage and, almost, your own leader, Honoric.' The others stare at you with fear and hatred in their eyes.

'I hope you slay him, for we can do nothing while he competes in the Ring,' says Maak.

Aiguchi walks on towards the woods accompanied by two legionaries. Then Maak steps forward. 'Come then, I shall explain the rules of the Ring of Vasch-Ro.' He hands you a map of the Ring, old and worn by the hands of many combatants. Maak goes on, 'In ages past a covenant was made between Vasch-Ro, the Wargod and Fate, Keeper of the Balance. Fate will turn her back on anyone who refuses the challenge of the Ring or crosses the Fatestones, the boundary of the Ring, before the contest is over. Let us begin.'

You are led to the wood ahead until you come to a stone gateway in its midst. Evenly spaced white stones stretch away to left and right. Maak says, 'This is the Victim's Gate, where you shall enter the Ring,' and he chuckles evilly. 'Aiguchi will be entering through the Victor's Gate. We shall be waiting to greet the winner who must exit the Ring from the Victor's Gate. Those white stones are the Fatestones, cross them at your peril. Well, I wish you ill-fortune, Avenger. May your bones rot for ever in the Ring.'

THE RING OF VASCH-RO

Hunter's Quarry

Victor's Gate

Path of Fools

Pillar of Death

Barrow Mound

Fatestones

Victim's Gate

The Duelwood

With that he leaves you alone to contemplate the weather-worn stone blocks that form the Victim's Gate. You step forward into the Ring, ready to do battle once more with a monk of the Scarlet Mantis, who is somewhere within. A path disappears into the wood ahead of you. Everything is quiet, save for the rustle of woodland animals and the quiet chatter of the birds. The air is still and heavy with musty odours.

Will you follow the Fatestones around to the north, all the way to the Victor's Gate? Turn to **34**.
Head through the Duelwood to the north-east? Turn to **48**.
Press on straight down the Path of Fools? Turn to **58**.
Head through the Duelwood to the south-east? Turn to **72**.
Follow the Fatestones around to the south, to the Victor's Gate? Turn to **82**.

71

You press on, picking up your torch and passing through the archway ahead. After a few yards a foul odour reaches your nostrils from up ahead, and strange snarling sounds echo down the tunnel. Rounding a bend in the tunnel you can see distant torchlight. Quickly you douse your own torch and edge your way silently towards the source of light. As you do so, the sound and smell grow stronger. Soon you are hidden in the shadows of the tunnel, looking into a large square room carved out of the rock. In its centre stands a large fire, smoke billowing up to be lost in the darkness above. Around it are arranged two long oak tables, strewn with all kinds of food and drink, mostly meat, half raw and half eaten. At the tables sit three hulking beasts dressed in greasy leather armour, with large wooden clubs at their side. They are gross and misshapen, their skin a greyish-green colour, warty and mottled. Their fat faces have wide splayed nostrils and rotting teeth. Their huge beards are matted with filth. You recognise them as Cave Trolls.

What interests you most is the blackened and stained livery they are wearing, for it is the stag with the spiral-horned antlers, the symbol of the Usurper. It seems these

Cave Trolls are in his service, kept out of harm's way down here but ready to be called upon if necessary. They are drinking heavily and arguing amongst themselves, their growling voices animal-like, barely discernible. Beyond them you can see another archway where the corridor continues. You can see no other exit. You must try to get through.

If you have the skill of Climbing you may try to climb upwards into the shadows and make your way around the cavern to the exit (turn to **94**). Otherwise, or if you do not wish to climb, you may sprint straight out to the fire and throw your flash powder onto it, and then sprint for the exit (turn to **102**).

72

You pass deeper into the Duelwood heading south-east, moving silently, using your training in woodcraft to the full and leaving virtually no trace of your passage. After a while you reach a small glade. Two bodies lie in its centre. They are previous combatants and it seems they both killed each other. One has buried its axe in the other's head, whilst it, in turn, has an old rusty sword lodged in its ribs. Their clothes are old and rotting and their eyeless skulls seem to grin in mock irony at the sky. Nearby you find an old satchel, presumably belonging to one of them. Much to your surprise, inside are small rubies and a few gold pieces. You may take these if you wish and note the Pouch of Rubies down on your Character Sheet. Turn to **82**.

73

On the next day you plunge deep into the forest, which is filled with beautiful trees and ferns. Majestic elms canopy the brown-leaved ground, dappled in sunshine. A leopard, unseen at first by you but not Glaivas, stares down from the crooked limb of a pine tree. Soon the ground becomes moist and mossy and the leaf carpet gives way to marsh marigolds and spider grass. Despite the beauty of your surroundings, a feeling of grim foreboding oppresses you. Glaivas shouts a sudden warning and you look round but the danger is from above. Another leopard lands on top of you, biting and raking with its claws. Lose 4 Endurance. You fall to the ground and then leap up as the leopard is on you again. Glaivas is bounding towards you. Will you try to block as the leopard springs (turn to **61**) or meet it with an Iron Fist punch (turn to **53**)?

74

You gain the foothills once more but the Golem of Flesh is not far behind. You flee east then north, towards the forested hills. Turn to **97**.

75

As Hazarbol and Mazarbol, the Devils of Twilight, spring you shout, almost panic-stricken as you clutch the Statuette, 'Dama, Shieldmaiden of the Gods, aid me!' If you have a Saint's Locket, turn to **30**. Otherwise nothing happens, so you decide to hurl your father's seal at his coat of arms and try to invoke his spirit. Turn to **90**.

76

You hurl yourself feet first in a slide at his legs but he is too quick and, hopping backwards and jabbing at your legs with his long spear, he gashes your thigh. Lose 2 Endurance. If you are still alive, you arch backwards into a handstand then spring lithely to your feet. Will you use the Winged Horse kick (turn to **145**) or an Iron Fist punch (turn to **117**)?

77

In the morning you feel much refreshed. You may restore up to 4 points of lost Endurance as Glaivas lays his healing fingers upon you. Turn to **414**.

78

You walk down dark side streets until you catch sight of the door to the inn on the east side of the city. A sign-written board above the door reads 'The Hostel from the Edge'. Inside is a huge, low vault filled with nigh on two hundred souls, less than half of whom are human. The non-humans are Orcs, Halvorcs and a group of dangerous looking Wolfen, erect and arrogant-looking. They have the heads of wolves and the bodies of beast-men but they stand over seven feet tall. Peasant girls are carrying tankards to the customers seated at low tables and benches, and a lame tramp lolls against the wall near the door. If you turn and leave straight away, turn to **6**. If you do not leave and you have a Yellow China Flower, turn to **221**. If not, you decide to sit yourself on a bench next to some unshaven young men who appear to have been drinking heavily (turn to **249**).

79

The movements of the Golem are slow but you are still exposing yourself to unnecessary risk using the Forked Lightning kick – it is not worth trying to fool this monster, but you drive your second strike towards the awful rictus grin that splits its face.

GOLEM OF FLESH
Defence against Forked Lightning kick: 5
Endurance: 25
Damage: 2 Dice

If you win, turn to **120**. If not your Defence against the swipes of its fists is 7. If you survive will you use the Forked Lightning kick again (return to the top of this paragraph), the Leaping Tiger kick (turn to **88**), the Tiger's Paw chop (turn to **99**) or the Iron Fist punch (turn to **108**)?

80

'You know what must be done,' says the Grandmaster, in his usual form once more. 'You must kill the Usurper and have yourself proclaimed rightful king of Irsmuncast. Evil forces are abroad once more in the Manmarch; the time has come for you to seek your new home. We do not expect to greet you on his peaceful island for many a long year.'

There is no feast to mark your going. You are to travel alone, incognito, so that the Usurper will not know to set defences against you. You bid the Grandmaster of the Dawn a sorrowful farewell and a spice trader bears you towards the Island of Plenty once more.

Turn to **15**.

81

You run on as the spears of the Halvorcs flatten the corn to either side of you, some quivering, their points buried in the ground. Soon they are flagging, but Glaivas is no more tired than you. Turn to **264**.

82

After a while you come to the edge of the wood. Beyond it is an open space with a large grassy knoll, the Barrow Mound. At its top rests a tall menhir, carved with ancient runes from top to bottom, the Pillar of Death. You circle the clearing, ears and eyes straining for any sight or sound of Aiguchi but you cannot find any trace of him. Will you move forward and examine the Mound closely (turn to **294**), climb the Mound and examine the Pillar (turn to **300**), follow the path north to the crossroads (turn to **273**), head north-east for the Victor's Gate (turn to **250**) or take this opportunity to cross the Fatestones and make good your escape from the Ring, heading for Irsmuncast (turn to **164**)?

83

As you run on, alert for any sign that you have been discovered and thankful that the Ranger is so stealthy, be tells you of the Spectral Company. They are nine, each once a Baron, lord of many men. They came from the city of Greydawn and worshipped the god of Empire, Moraine. They were the nine generals who led the men of Greydawn in search of Empire, on a quest to conquer the Valley of the Lich-Kings, which in those days was called the Valley of Grain. The Fleshless King was newly returned from the dead and, still active those centuries ago, he rode at the head of his troops. The power of his magic cast down the generals and he took them to be his servants, killing them and bringing their tormented bodies back to life. Now, in the form of spectres which can suck a man's life from him with a touch, they cow everyone in the valley. Their leader, Ganarre, is a powerful sorcerer, the Fleshless King's brother, differing from him only in that his body has retained its cloak of flesh and the fact that a part of his brain festered many centuries ago. Turn to **106**.

84

Radziwil throws the chess table into your face and a burning flame spurts from Elektra's outstretched hands, searing you so that you fall to the floor. You are soon on your feet but Radziwil denounces you as a traitor and orders you killed in the name of the Usurper. He is one of the tyrant's secret informers and you are soon surrounded by the Usurper's soldiers and the powerful priesthood of Nemesis, for this is their place. Even for Avenger there is no escape.

85

You reach a ledge below an unclimbable wall of rock that leads to the summit, after a difficult exertion, and wait. After a couple of hours you can hear an occasional scraping below. Looking down the giddying drop, you can see the bald head of the Golem climbing ponderously up to meet you. You search for rocks to drop on it, but the rock face is hard and yields no chunks of debris. There is no other way down so you use your shuriken, aiming at its head. By the time it hauls itself over the ledge it wears a crown of three throwing stars but they do not seem to affect it. There is little room to move and at last you run out of the strength to resist. The Golem picks you up above its head and hurls you down the mountainside to your death.

86

As your blow lands there is a faint noise, like the Death-Knell of the great bell in the Iron-city of Dis, deep in the Underworld. The Fiend seems to stagger but is unwounded. If this is the third time you have heard the Death-Knell turn to **66**. Otherwise, will you try a Winged Horse kick (turn to **163**), a Dragon's Tail throw (turn to **178**), a Cobra Strike punch (turn to **156**) or the skill of Yubi-Jutsu if you have it (turn to **93**), or flee, leaving Glaivas on his own (turn to **201**)? You may only attempt a punch or kick if you have Inner Force left.

87

You have been bitten by a Werewolf. With a thrill of horror, you realise that you almost certainly caught the disease of Lycanthropy. You are doomed to become a wolf at every full moon, unless you can find some kind of cure. Note down on your Character Sheet that you are a Werewolf. However, you will not be affected for some time yet. Grimly you resolve to carry out your mission before turning your mind to this problem. Turn to **71**.

88

The monster appears to be dull-witted and your leap takes it by surprise.

GOLEM OF FLESH
Defence against Leaping Tiger kick: 4
Endurance: 25
Damage: 2 Dice

If you win, turn to **120**. If not your Defence against the swipe of its fists is 9. If you survive will you use the Leaping Tiger kick again (return to the top of this paragraph), the Forked Lightning kick (turn to **79**), the Tiger's Paw chop (turn to **99**) or the Iron Fist punch (turn to **108**)?

89

You step forward and unleash a Winged Horse kick at Aiguchi's face. However, he is too quick and he sidesteps it and then brings the nunchaku down across your shin, cracking it painfully. Lose 3 Endurance. If you are still alive, you hop backwards out of range. Will you try the Cobra Strike (turn to **303**) or the Whirlpool throw (turn to **46**)?

90

The seal clatters against the coat of arms. 'Father, Loremaster, save me.' But nothing can save you now. The Devils close in around you and together they are too strong. Perhaps Astaroth alone could have killed you, you will never know, but it is his jaws which tear your head from your shoulders at the last, and Scourge takes your soul down to the lowest circle of hell where he will torture you for all eternity.

91

Using your garrotte you silently choke one of the orcish overseers and you both slip under a canvas awning which flaps in the night wind. There are no slaves using it for shelter, so Glaivas takes the opportunity to tell you of the Spectral Company. They are nine, each once a Baron, lord of many men. They came from the city of Greydawn and worshipped the god of Empire, Moraine. They were the nine generals who led the men of Greydawn in search of Empire, on a quest to conquer the Valley of the Lich-Kings, which in those days was called the Valley of Grain. The Fleshless King was newly returned from the dead and, still active those centuries ago, he rode at the head of his troops. The power of his magic cast down the generals and he took them to be his servants, killing them and bringing their tormented bodies back to life. Now, in the form of spectres which can suck a man's life from him with a touch, they cow everyone in the valley. Their leader, Ganarre, is a powerful sorcerer, the Fleshless King's brother, differing from him only in that his body has retained its cloak of flesh and the fact that part of his brain festered many centuries ago. Turn to **115**.

92

An arrow slams into your shoulder. Lose 4 Endurance. If you are still alive, you stagger back quickly in pain. Aiguchi almost has another arrow nocked to his bow. Will you run at Aiguchi, weaving as you go (turn to **124**), drop flat on the long grass and try to creep up on Aiguchi (turn to **135**) or drop flat into the long grass and crawl across the Fatestones, out of the Ring of Vasch-Ro, and make good your escape (turn to **164**)?

93

The Fiend is not built like a man but it may once have been one. You can only hope that the point you are aiming for with your Cobra Strike is a vital nerve centre, as its horned arms scissor towards your neck.

FIEND FROM THE PIT
Defence against Yubi-Jutsu: 7
Endurance: —
Damage: 2 Dice

If you hit it successfully, turn to **86**. If you failed you must try to dodge the monster's scything horn-tipped arms. Your Defence is 5. If you are still alive you may try the Dragon's Tail throw (turn to **178**), a Winged Horse kick (turn to **163**), a regular Cobra Strike punch (turn to **156**) or use your skill of Yubi-Jutsu again (return to the top of this paragraph), or flee, leaving Glaivas on his own (turn to **201**). You may only attempt a regular punch or kick if you have Inner Force left.

94

As quickly as possible you strap on the cat's claws and inch your way up the wall. Soon you are lost to sight in the shadow, your keen night vision enabling you to make your way around the chamber. You have almost reached the exit when you realise the three Cave Trolls are looking about, puzzled expressions on their ugly faces. They are sniffing the air. To your horror you realise they have smelt you and you hurry on, crawling like a fly. But it is to no avail, they have pinpointed your position by smell alone and they lumber over towards you. You are directly above the archway now. If you have the skill of Acrobatics, you may try to drop to the floor below and into the archway where they will only be able to come at you one at a time (turn to **107**). Otherwise you have no choice but to roll to the archway as best you can. Turn to **118**.

95

The bodies of the Halvorcs lie all around you in the corn. Glaivas wipes his sword dry and you climb the Palisade of Thorns to find a barren heathland beyond. Turn to **69**.

96

You wait on the wooden roof of a nearby house after climbing up its low veranda until beyond midnight. You manage, using your grappling hook and rope, to climb the garden wall but a dog scents you and there is a cacophony of barking. Soon the garden is swarming with guards. To continue would be near-certain death so you slip back down the wall and away into the night, climbing onto the roof of another large building where you sleep the night away.

In the morning you awake to the realisation that you have slept atop the army barracks. Soldiers, men and Halvorcs and Orcs, drill in separate parties until evening, making it difficult to move, so you bide your time, noting that the Halvorcs show commendable discipline. What you can see of the city appears to be somewhat under the heel of the Usurper's loyal troops. At evening you are able to descend safely to the street and you search for an inn where you may better gauge the mood of the citizenry. Turn to **401**.

97

The Golem pursues you relentlessly and your body is nearing exhaustion as you stagger on through the wooded hills. Lose 2 Endurance. If you are still alive, you feel as if you are in the middle of a terrible nightmare as you force yourself onwards, oblivious to the pain in your lungs and the blisters on your feet. At last as dusk approaches, you stumble away from the hills towards a barren and desolate valley. Ahead in the far distance is a black wall of rock. Suddenly, awareness stops you in your tracks. You are in the most dangerous region of all Orb, approaching the Rift, the Bowels of Orb, where much of the evil that affects the land boils forth from lightless pits near the centre of the world. If you have received insight about this area through prayer, turn to **4**. Otherwise, make a Fate Roll. If Fate smiles on you, turn to **52**. If Fate turns her back on you, turn to **23**.

98

Radziwil says, 'But don't you think things should change?' You look blankly at him and he falls to thinking about his next move. Elektra watches you through lowered eyelids. You pay the price for your conservative opening – Radziwil is a skilled player and your thoughts are distracted. You are lucky to gain a draw. Will you say goodbye and leave now (turn to **6**), or change your mind and quietly say that you believe the tyranny of the Usurper must be overthrown at any cost (turn to **84**)?

99

You chop with the side of your hand at one of the seams of flesh from which the sickly-sweet ooze is running in an effort to split it asunder. You may add 2 to the damage done if you succeed.

GOLEM OF FLESH
Defence against Tiger's Paw chop: 4
Endurance: 25
Damage: 2 Dice

If you win, turn to **120**. If not your Defence against the swipe of its fists is 9.

If you survive will you use the Tiger's Paw chop again (return to the top of this paragraph), the Forked Lightning kick (turn to **79**), the Leaping Tiger kick (turn to **88**) or the Iron Fist punch (turn to **108**)?

As the silk flag flutters down to the tower roof you walk to the battlements and look out over the panorama of the city. You can clearly see Force-Lady Gwyneth on a grey warhorse apparently inspecting her troops. They are arranged in serried ranks on the parade ground beyond Cross Street. The majority are women dressed in chainmail but a sizeable number of men, too, carry the lozenge-shaped shields of Dama. A few are in full plate armour, their faces bidden behind visors. A small detachment of Halvorcs and men bearing the Usurper's stag emblem slouch nearby, at ease. Gwyneth's lieutenant points up at you and the trumpeter sounds five short notes. Gwyneth shouts a command and the shieldmaidens divide into two, half marching towards the Palace and half towards the army barracks.

The detachment of Halvorcs and men react slowly – many have fallen to quick sword thrusts before they realise that the revolt has begun. Then they flee. The skill at arms of Gwyneth's warriors is a joy to behold as they meet the Usurper's men in open battle on the streets below. They are reinforced by the monks of Kwon and for some time the fighting sways back and forth, but the warrior-women are outnumbered and their advance is halted before the Palace gates. Looking down to Cross Street you can see that the barracks is holding out and a group of priests are leaving the temple to Nemesis, marching to the relief of the army. The battle hangs in the balance. There is nothing you can do but watch. It would be foolish to fight your way out through the Palace.

The rabble has not risen to throw off the yoke of oppression. If the Shogun Kiyamo of the Island of Plenty gave you a hundred samurai under the order of Onikaba, and you ordered them to journey to Doomover and across the Manmarch, turn to **399**. If he did not, or if you ordered them through the Valley of the Lich-Kings, turn to **410**.

You attack the devils as they spring upon you in the following order. First Hazarbol, his jaws dripping with bile;

then Mazarbol, his insane laughter threatening your sanity; then Scourge with the flashing hooves of iron; and finally Astaroth. Each time the Dagger sinks into a devil's flesh the rune glows brighter, the blade shrieks and the devil is banished back to hell. After you defeat a devil make another Fate Roll for the next in order. Subtract 1 from the dice if you are attacking Astaroth for Fate cannot control his destiny fully. If Fate turns her back on you, turn to **112** but if she continues to smile on you, another devil is banished. If you banish Astaroth, turn to **189**.

102

Without a moment's hesitation, you take your powder in one hand and sprint into the room, directly towards the fire. The Cave Trolls surge up from their seats in astonishment, bellowing and howling in apparent glee at what they see as their next meal offering itself up to them. But they are too slow to prevent you reaching the fire and you hurl the dust (cross it from your Character Sheet) averting your eyes as you do so.

There is a blinding flash and you sprint on. The Cave Trolls are lumbering about, hands pressed to their eyes, moaning in pain. You reach the archway and turn to face them where only one can reach you at a time. Your ruse has worked perfectly. After a few seconds, they regain their sight and lope towards you, howling in rage, beating the ground with their clubs. When their slow-witted minds have registered the fact that they can't all attack you at once they come to a stop and look at each other dully. The largest, a great hulking brute, smiling horribly to reveal yellow tusks, shuffles up to you swinging his enormous club as if it were a match.

It will not be possible to throw the Cave Troll in this limited space, nor do you think it likely you could anyway, due to its great size and weight. But you can try a Tiger's Paw chop (turn to **134**) or a Leaping Tiger kick (turn to **140**). Alternatively if you have the skill of Yubi-Jutsu and wish to use it, turn to **150**.

103

You are not fast enough and the arrow slams into your shoulder before you can knock it aside. Lose 4 Endurance. If you are still alive, you stagger back quickly in pain. Aiguchi has almost nocked another arrow to his bow. Will you run at Aiguchi, weaving as you go (turn to **124**), drop flat in the long grass and try to creep up on Aiguchi (turn to **135**) or drop flat into the long grass and crawl across the Fatestones, out of the Ring of Vasch-Ro, and make good your escape (turn to **164**)?

104

The root tastes bitter but its juices have an immediate effect, seeming to muddy your thoughts. You decide to try to find the Spirit Tiger on the spirit plane. The leaves are still swirling in the chill wind. Will you try to project your mind into the spirit plane by force of will (turn to **143**) or meditate and try to set your mind free from the shackles of your body (turn to **152**)?

105

The sign showing a single violet flame hangs in a narrow thoroughfare called Iskra Street. You walk up wide stairs into a large club room with a spinet at one end. It could be used for dancing but a great many soldiers, priests and priestesses lounge on divans drinking wine. The serving wenches are polite and dressed in uniforms of black velvet and silver satin. There is absolute silence and all heads turn as you walk in – you could hear a sparrow breathing. Without exception the priests and priestesses sport the whirlpool symbol and most wear black. They are all human. If you decide you have made a mistake in coming here and leave, turn to **6**. If you pluck up courage to sit alone at a low chess table, turn to **19**.

106

As you run on, unflagging, a faint but doleful cry is borne to you on the wings of the night wind. You look to Glaivas in the starlight and he says, 'That was no mortal cry, that is the cry of the Sylph, imprisoned in the great Keystone above the West Gate of the City of the Runes of Doom. It is a signal that Ganarre leads the Spectral Company forth tonight.' Glaivas gives you a small crystal vial. 'It is holy water, blessed in the name of the All-Mother. Cast it at the faces of the undead at need.' You swallow nervously at the grim expression on the Ranger's face. 'We could turn north, towards the mountains,' he suggests. Will you turn north (turn to **123**) or continue east (turn to **131**)?

107

You let go your grip on the wall and topple backwards into a sky-diving flip, to land nimbly on your feet. The Cave Trolls gape in astonishment and then bellow and howl at the sight of you, smashing their clubs against the ground and loping towards you. You dart into the archway and turn to face them in a martial stance of the Way of the Tiger. Only one of them will be able to attack you at a time. At this show of defence they look at each other and then the largest, a great hulking brute, smiling horribly, revealing yellow tusks, shuffles up to you, swinging his enormous club as if it were a match. It will not be possible to throw the Cave Troll in this limited space, nor do you think it likely you could anyway, due to its great size and weight. But you can try a Tiger's Paw chop (turn to **134**) or a Leaping Tiger kick (turn to **140**). Alternatively if you have the skill of Yubi-Jutsu and wish to use it, turn to **150**.

108

You stand up to the towering hulk of cobbled-together flesh, ready to trade blow for blow.

GOLEM OF FLESH
Defence against Iron Fist punch: 4
Endurance: 25
Damage: 2 Dice

If you win, turn to **120**. If not your Defence against the swipe of its fists is 9. If you survive will you use the Iron Fist punch again (return to the top of this paragraph), the Forked Lightning kick (turn to **79**), the Tiger's Paw chop (turn to **99**) or the Leaping Tiger kick (turn to **88**)?

109

You saunter back down the main street, Palace Road, and down another wide street called Cross Street. Three temples line it. On one side is a great church too tall for its width with great archways ringing a cloister forty feet above the street, and four towers with turrets shaped like flames piercing the sky. From the look of the priests talking outside you guess it is the Temple to Nemesis, the Supreme Principle of Evil. On the other side is a small chapel in the shape of a Cross, with a steeple and spire topped by the Cross of Avatar, Supreme Principle of Good. Beyond it is a very large church of grey stone looking as much like a square-towered fort as a church with a central pyramid. It flies a flag showing a warrior woman, holding a sword aloft, with a lozenge-shaped shield resting on the ground before her. The lanterns which line Cross Street make the large churches look forbidding. The Temple to Avatar is locked up so you search for someone who may tell you the whereabouts of the Temple to Kwon. A tall woman accounted in chainmail and sword steps out of the grey stone church while a tramp pads towards you. Is no city without its poor, you wonder? Will you ignore the tramp and talk to the tall woman (turn to **359**), or give the tramp some gold (turn to **216**)?

You lose sight of the figures but decide to head into the heart of the hills. As you enter the basin between them a great column of fire reaches forty feet towards the sky before you. The glare shows a sight that chills you with fear. Standing atop each of the hills which encircle you are two Spectral Knights. You are surrounded by the Spectral Company. Before you is a well and behind it stands Ganarre, eldritch brother of the Fleshless King. They begin to chant, drawing power from the shrine that was built many millennia ago, below the well. All will to resist leaves you and the Spectral Company close slowly in, to deprive you of life with their icy touch.

You turn north together and lope towards a horizon where low hills are swathed in a blue-green haze of forest. Glaivas covers the ground as quickly and untiringly as you and you settle down for the night at the forest's edge. He tells you that, like many forests, the Forest of Arkadan brings its dangers but that, with his guidance, you should avoid most of them. He cautions you that should you become lost you must head north, towards the Mountains of Horn, before turning east, and at all costs avoid the Crypts of Arkadan at the forest's heart. Your night is troubled by dark dreams; the malice of the gods of evil seems to be withering your heart, turning its edges black and dead. As you sleep, your mind fills with a vision of a gigantic black bubbling cauldron, inside which some unnatural Fiend is being brewed by mighty and dark minds. Turn to **73**.

You attack the devils as they spring upon you in the following order. First Hazarbol, his jaws dripping with bile; then Mazarbol, his insane laughter threatening your sanity; then Scourge with the flashing hooves of iron; and finally Astaroth. If Fate turns her back on you while you are fighting Hazarbol or Mazarbol you lose 6 Endurance due to their raking steel claws. If you are fighting Scourge when Fate turns her back on you, his iron hooves pound your back and you lose 8 Endurance. If Astaroth is your foe when you run out of luck, his jaws close around you and you lose 10 Endurance. If you are still alive you must attack the same devil again. Make another Fate Roll. Subtract 1 from the dice if you are attacking Astaroth for Fate cannot control his destiny fully. If your luck changes and Fate smiles on you, turn to **101**. If not return to the top of this paragraph.

113

At the last minute, you step to the side and whip your right arm across, snatching the arrow right out of the air, an act of pure reflex. Turning to face Aiguchi, you snap it in two like a twig. Aiguchi stands stock still in amazement, but you cannot make out the muffled curse as he mutters to himself. 'Impressive, ninja!' he shouts, 'but I am a Master of Weapons,' and he throws down his bow and quiver and picks up his curve-bladed spear, the naginata. He then executes a mind-boggling series of movements, as if he were fighting several opponents at once. The naginata is almost a blur as he thrusts and parries, performing a complex but deadly dance. You can see that he is very, very fast, but is he as fast as you? Then he begins to edge towards you, crab-like, the tip of his spear always pointed, unerringly, at your throat. You circle each other. Suddenly he hops and thrusts the spear at your belly with great speed, but you sweep it aside with your arm. For a brief moment you are inside the reach of the naginata. If you have the skill of Yubi-Jutsu, you realise he is too quick for you to use a precision nerve-strike, and you will have to slow him down first. Will you try the Leaping Tiger kick (turn to **56**), the Teeth of the Tiger throw (turn to **22**), a Tiger's Paw chop (turn to **38**) or wait for a suitable moment and, using Inner Force, attempt to snap Aiguchi's naginata (turn to **10**)?

114

Glaivas runs on seeing his way through the close-set trees with owl eyes and weaving like an antelope. You follow just as quickly until at last a deep black pool appears in the lea of a small cliff. Without hesitation he dives in and you follow. There is a hissing of steam as you meet the icy water but the pain and the throbbing heat die away. There are no trees to cover you here though and the Fiend swoops down on you with a scream of delight and soul-lust. You swim for the muddy bank when there is a commotion all around you. Small swift shapes are launching themselves at the Fiend. Glaivas climbs out and shouts at you to follow him. You run on, listening to shrill cackles and the howls of the frustrated Fiend behind you. You run on and on until dawn, when, to your surprise, you find yourself at the edge of the Forest of Arkadan. Glaivas turns to you and says, 'We can but hope that the pain of the spiritwrack which afflicted the Fiend on this plane has driven it back to hell.' Sure enough you rest for a while, free from the brooding sense of doom that troubled you so recently.

In the morning Glaivas explains his guess that the Fiend from the Pit was confused by the Forest-Sprites, themselves magical and able to harm the monster. Eventually it could bear the pain of being on the plane of life, or Orb, no longer. The Forest-Sprites have paid off their debt to the Ranger-Lord. You press on soon after sunrise. Turn to **414**.

115

As you crouch still beneath the awning, a faint but doleful cry is borne to you on the wings of the night wind. You look to Glaivas in the starlight and he says, 'That was no mortal cry, that is the cry of the Sylph, imprisoned in the great Keystone above the West Gate of the City of the Runes of Doom. It is a signal that Ganarre leads the Spectral Company forth tonight.' Glaivas gives you a small crystal vial. 'It is holy water, blessed in the name of the All-Mother. Cast it at the faces of the undead at need.' You swallow nervously at the grim expression on the Ranger's face.

There is a splat-splat of naked footsteps in the mud and a girl child of about fifty or so seasons squirms under the awning, looking fearfully over her shoulder for any signs of pursuit as she does so. Your eyes, as sharp as an owl's in the gloom, pick out her scrawny form and the squalid, torn and muddied sackcloth tunic, inadequate protection against the cold of the night. She cannot see in the gloom and she begins to sob quietly, oblivious of your presence. Will you nudge Glaivas in the ribs and motion that you wish to leave (turn to **146**) or speak to the slave girl (turn to **154**)?

116

With a yell that shatters the stillness of the night you leap for the whirlwind of leaves and drive your leg upwards, kicking with the strength of a mule. You meet no resistance and sail through the whirlwind, but as you go, your stomach churns as a black mind of pure evil touches your soul. The whirlpool begins to die down. Will you eat the mandrake root and try to call the Spirit Tiger (turn to **167**) or walk towards Glaivas and wait to see what happens (turn to **128**)?

117

As Aiguchi sweeps the naginata down at you, you step in and, taking the blow on your left forearm, drive your right fist at his face.

AIGUCHI THE WEAPONMASTER
Defence against Iron Fist punch: 6
Endurance: 9
Damage: 2 Dice

If you have defeated him, turn to **309**. If he is still alive he drops to one knee and aims a wicked thrust at your abdomen. Your Defence is 7. If you are still alive, will you use the Iron Fist punch again (return to the top of this paragraph), the Winged Horse kick (turn to **145**) or a Dragon's Tail throw (turn to **76**)?

118

You scramble down the wall in front of the exit and the Cave Trolls bellow and howl at the sight of you, smashing their clubs against the ground and loping forward. As you land on the ground one of them hurls a large stool at you, sending you sprawling back into the archway. Lose 3 Endurance. If you are still alive, you leap to your feet and prepare to defend yourself where only one of them can reach you at a time. At this show of defence they look at each other and then the largest, a great hulking brute, smiling horribly to reveal yellow tusks, shuffles up to you swinging his enormous club as if it were a match. It will not be possible to throw the Cave Troll in this limited space, nor do you think it likely you could anyway, due to its great size and weight. But you can try a Tiger's Paw chop (turn to **134**) or a Leaping Tiger kick (turn to **140**). Alternatively if you have the skill of Yubi-Jutsu and wish to use it turn to **150**.

119

'And what of I?' says the figure. 'I would have killed you out-of-hand had you not declared yourself.' Will you take this as a challenge and reply with a throwing star (turn to **274**) or will you ask him what brings him to the Bowels of Orb (turn to **43**)?

120

Your last blow stops the Golem in its tracks. It rocks slightly from side to side then collapses, first on one knee, then its forehead bows slowly to the ground. You step back, breathing deeply, then the Golem disappears. Where a moment since it was bowed in an absurd posture of supplication, there is no more than mist. Then a figure, arms outstretched towards you, sways out of the mist. It is the Golem of Flesh and it bears no sign of the damage you inflicted on its patchwork body! It speaks again in its cracked hoarse voice, 'My name is Everyman and I am Legion.' Your skin crawls with horror as you realise you must either flee or fight it again. Will you flee (turn to **230**), attack using the Winged Horse kick (turn to **139**), the Leaping Tiger kick (turn to **149**) or the Tiger's Paw chop (turn to **158**)?

121

As soon as you pull out the Dagger, the rune on it begins to glow brightly. Astaroth can call forth no more devils to aid him but your foes are already very mighty, while you have no skill with a dagger. You are in the lap of Fate and as you try to stab each devil you must make a Fate Roll. If Fate smiles on you on this your first roll, turn to **101**. If Fate turns her back on you, turn to **112**.

122

Glaivas runs on seeing his way through the close-set trees with owl eyes and weaving like an antelope. You follow just as quickly until at last a deep black pool appears in the lea of a small cliff. Without hesitation, he dives in and you follow. There is a hissing of steam as you meet the icy water but the pain and the throbbing heat die away. There are no trees to cover you here though and the Fiend swoops down on you with a scream of delight and soul-lust. You swim for the muddy bank but slip in the ooze and the Fiend from the Pit crushes you in a horned embrace. All goes dark around you, then the terrible ringing of the great bell of Dis the Iron-city of the Underworld reverberates around your skull. All around you is cold iron. You have been carried away to hell where you will suffer eternal torment.

123

You run for many miles towards the mountains which tower blackly above you. Your acute sense of hearing picks up the sound of distant hoofbeats and a chill runs down your back. You tell Glaivas that there are four horses approaching and he says, 'They have found us. We must make a stand.' You climb quickly towards a narrow canyon mouth, flanked by sheer cliffs, and wait. Turn to **284**.

124

You run at Aiguchi, dodging and weaving, but the rate at which he is able to let fly an arrow and nock another to his bow is phenomenal, as is his accuracy. He is a Master of the Bow. Arrows fly at you, only seconds apart. Slowed by your wound, you cannot cope with them all. First one and then another and another embed themselves in your body and moments later you are dead.

125

You press on using Glaivas' map and see no more of the Ranger. On the next day the assassin tries to strike again but you hear him and escape. Some days later, however, you are not so lucky. Having passed a cairn of skulls, you enter a vast plain of wheat, where men and women are tolling under the whips of orcish overseers.

That night your senses alert you to danger, but it is too late. The Spectral Company have come for your soul. Grey figures approach on horseback and you quicken your pace towards a circle of hills. Turn to **110**.

126

You are too slow and the shaft of the naginata whips under your outstretched arms and slams into your ribs, bowling you over. Lose 2 Endurance.

If you are still alive, you roll to your feet to be greeted by Aiguchi smiling at his success. Will you try to throw Aiguchi using the Teeth of the Tiger throw (turn to **22**), punch him with a Tiger's Paw chop (turn to **38**), kick him using the Leaping Tiger kick (turn to **56**) or try again to break his naginata (turn to **10**)?

127

You run towards the figure and it spurs its horse forward, drawing its bastard sword which glows with a silver radiance. You dodge aside and unleash a Leaping Tiger kick. Turn to **262**.

128

Glaivas walks to meet you, and together you watch as the whirlpool of leaves dies down and in its place a great bat-winged figure, the loathsome Fiend of your dreams, takes shape. Will you eat the mandrake root and try to call the Spirit Tiger (turn to **192**), flee into the forest hoping that the Fiend will either lose you or attack Glaivas (turn to **201**), or move in to attack with Glaivas whose sword is ready (turn to **283**)?

'Speak the vow taken by those who worship Innoka whom I would be glad to call my friends.' The voice sounds like that of a young man. The language is the common tongue but his accent is like none you have ever heard. You have no idea of the vow taken by those who worship Innoka. Will you make a break towards a patch of dense forest (turn to **301**) or admit that you do not know the vow (turn to **171**)?

Golspiel becomes a little vague concerning the possible dispositions of his mercenaries. He finishes by saying that he will leave things up to Antocidas the One-Eyed, his capable general, and gives you a bracelet of red coral as a token of his support. Note the Red Coral on your Character Sheet. He tells you he is due to meet one of the Usurper's captains, so you bow and take your leave.

If you wish to approach another faction with whom you have not yet spoken, will it be the Swordswomen of Dama, Shieldmaiden of the Gods (turn to **296**), the priesthood of Time (turn to **394**) or the rabble of the city (turn to **68**)? If you feel you have the support you need, you make your final preparations to assassinate the Usurper (turn to **9**).

You run on across the flat fields towards a ring of low hills which marks the edge of the wilderness. As you near the hills you have a premonition of doom. Glaivas points and the moon briefly shows four dark figures approaching the hills. 'It is the Spectral Company,' he whispers. 'We must turn north.' Will you turn north (turn to **123**) or try to surprise them and give battle (turn to **110**)?

You tell Glaivas that you cannot reach the spirit plane and that you must save yourselves without the Spirit Tiger's help. You can hear the Fiend settling on the trees above and your body feels as if it is about to burst into flame. Lose 4 Endurance.

If you are still alive, Glaivas whispers, 'Follow me, all we can do is try to reach water.' You stagger on, your flesh burning, as Glaivas leads you with unerring skill through the deep forest night. As you curve downhill and the ground becomes springy and damp underfoot there is another bloodcurdling howl and the temperature within you rises still further.

If a leopard has been killed in the Forest of Arkadan turn to **122**. If not turn to **114**.

133

It is not hard to follow Glaivas' tracks through the corn and soon you hear his voice urging you to get down, as the blackhawk circles above you once more. He had been tracking you and you have met close to the thorn hedge. It is not long before another group of Halvorcs runs towards you. Glaivas springs up beckoning for you to follow. Turn to **353**.

134

You dart in under the sweeping blows of the Troll and chop your hand at the huge Troll's ribs.

CAVE TROLL
Defence against Tiger's Paw chop: 4
Endurance: 20
Damage: 2 Dice + 2

If you reduce the Troll to 8 or less Endurance turn to **170**. If it is at 9 or more Endurance, it tries to crush you in its tree-trunk-like arms. Your Defence is 9, as you dodge its sluggish attack. If you are still alive will you punch again (return to the top of the paragraph) or try a kick (turn to **140**)?

135

You throw yourself at the ground, moving away from the spot you were at immediately. Using your superb training you are able to crawl around Aiguchi without giving away your position, holding yourself stock still when he looks in your direction. Aiguchi becomes increasingly worried, backing slowly to the quarry. Soon you have worked your way to his rear, but he has backed out of the long grass onto the stony ground of the rim of the quarry.

Will you wait until his back is turned and hurl a shuriken (turn to **415**) or (if you have the skill of Poison Needles) try to spit a poison needle at him although he is at extreme range (turn to **148**) or try to dart silently up behind him (turn to **173**)?

136

You tell Glaivas that you feel you must push on along the road, that too much time will be wasted in the Forest of Arkadan. He replies that he knows these lands and there will be perils enough even for two. 'If you go on along the roads I will be powerless to help you against the Assassin's Guild and the Spectral Company. Perhaps you are not a mortal but a god.'

With that he turns his back and walks away. Will you press on into the Valley of the Lich-Kings (turn to **125**) or say that you bow to his greater knowledge and ask him to take you to Arkadan (turn to **111**)?

137

The figure is silent and unmoving once more. Then it tilts back the sunburst helmet to reveal a face whose handsomeness takes you by surprise. It is disarmingly boyish, blue eyes in a bronzed face, framed with flaxen ringlets. It seems altogether improbable that such a man should be astride this magnificent charger on the edge of the Rift.

'I have never heard of such an island but I sense that there is no evil in you.'

You ask him what brings him to the Bowels of Orb. Turn to **43**.

138

Golspiel accepts your bribe and then gives you an Amber Pendant as a token of his support. Note the exchange of items on your Character Sheet. He does not refer to your 'gift' after thanking you and you ask him about the dispositions of his mercenary force, but he says, 'I leave that up to my general, Antocidas the One-Eyed, he is very able. I'm due to meet one of the Usurper's captains now, it might be embarrassing if he found you here.' You agree and take your leave.

If you wish to approach another faction with whom you have not yet spoken, will it be the Swordswomen of Dama, Shieldmaiden of the Gods (turn to **296**), the priesthood of the Temple to Time (turn to **394**) or the rabble of the city (turn to **68**)? If you feel you have the support you need, you make your final preparations to assassinate the Usurper (turn to **9**).

139

The monster moves ponderously as before as you spin and drive your foot at its midriff.

GOLEM OF FLESH
Defence against Winged Horse kick: 9
Endurance: 25
Damage: 2 Dice

If you win, turn to **211**. Otherwise the Golem flails at you with its knotted fists once more. You are beginning to tire and your Defence as you try to dodge is 7. If you survive, will you use the Winged Horse kick again (return to the top of this paragraph), the Leaping Tiger kick (turn to **149**) or the Tiger's Paw chop (turn to **158**)?

140

The bulky Troll aims a ponderous blow at your head. You duck under it easily and then leap up, lashing the ball of your foot at its throat.

CAVE TROLL
Defence against Leaping Tiger kick: 5
Endurance: 20
Damage: 2 Dice + 2

If you reduce the Troll to 8 or less Endurance turn to **170**. If it is at 9 or more Endurance, it tries to crush you under its great club. Your Defence is 8, as you dodge its sluggish attack.

    If you are still alive, will you kick again (return to the top of this paragraph) or try a punch (turn to **134**)?

141

There is a howl of glee from the figure. 'Then die!' it shouts, drawing the huge bastard sword from its back and charging you. You dodge and use a Leaping Tiger kick to knock it from the saddle. The sword glows with a silver radiance. Turn to **262**.

142

The rock face becomes almost sheer and you struggle to find enough hand and footholds, your limbs aching with the strain. You overstretch yourself and your feet swing away from the rock over a thousand foot drop. Make a Fate Roll. If Fate smiles on you, turn to **42**. If Fate turns her back on you, turn to **29**.

143

You still your heart and try to project your mind onto the spirit plane but its stays firmly rooted within your body and as you watch the whirlpool of leaves dies down. In its place a great bat-winged shadow, the loathsome Fiend you saw in your dreams, takes shape. Will you flee into the forest hoping the Fiend will either lose you or attack Glaivas (turn to **201**) or move in to attack it as Glaivas draws his sword (turn to **283**)?

144

You climb out over the Palisade of Thorns once more and decide to hide in the reeds near the river you crossed earlier. Glaivas does not reappear, so you skirt the Palisade at night, a long detour, and set out east across the heath. You travel only at night and make good progress until, on the second night, your heightened senses warn you of supernatural evil.

Grey figures on horseback appear on the horizon to the south and you quicken your pace towards a circle of hills. Turn to **110**.

145

As Aiguchi thrusts, you grab his naginata just below the blade and leap into the air, unleashing a flying Winged Horse kick at his head.

AIGUCHI THE WEAPONMASTER
Defence against Winged Horse kick: 7
Endurance: 9
Damage: 2 Dice

If you have beaten him, turn to **309**. If he is still alive he uses the naginata like a quarterstaff, driving the shaft of the spear at your throat as you land on your feet. Your Defence is 7. If you are still alive, will you kick again (return to the top of this paragraph), try the Iron Fist punch (turn to **117**) or a Dragon's Tail throw (turn to **76**)?

146

Glaivas nods. The sobbing girl does not even notice as you roll from under the awning and vanish unseen into the night. The Ranger says, 'Should we turn north, towards the mountains?' Will you turn north (turn to **123**) or continue east (turn to **131**)?

147

Try as you might, you are unable to contact the spirit plane, your mind remains firmly rooted in your body. You can hear the Fiend settling on the branches above you and your body feels as if it is about to explode into flame. Lose 4 Endurance. If you are still alive, Glaivas whispers, 'Follow me, all we can do is try to reach water.' You stagger on, your flesh burning, as Glaivas leads with unerring skill through the deep forest night. As you curve downhill and the ground becomes springy and damp underfoot there is another bloodcurdling howl and the temperature within you rises still further. If a leopard has been killed in the Forest of Arkadan turn to **122**. If not turn to **114**.

You place a needle on your tongue and, edging a little closer, spit it at him as hard as you can. It flies through the air towards him, just as the sound of rushing air causes him to turn his head. Make a Fate Roll, but apply −4 to your Fate Modifier for this roll only, due to the range. If you succeed, turn to **245**. If you fail, turn to **258**.

149

Your leap surprises the dull-witted Golem.

GOLEM OF FLESH
Defence against Leaping Tiger kick: 4
Endurance: 25
Damage: 2 Dice

If you win, turn to **211**. Otherwise you are tiring and your Defence as you duck is 7. If you survive will you use the Leaping Tiger kick again (return to the top of this paragraph), the Winged Horse kick (turn to **139**) or the Tiger's Paw chop (turn to **158**)?

150

Hoping that the nervous structure of these creatures is not too different from that of a human, you wait for an opportunity to deliver a nerve-strike. The huge Troll swings its club in an arc aimed at your head. You duck under the ponderous blow and the club slams into the tunnel wall with a reverberating thud. You leap up and drive the ball of your foot at the beast's throat with unerring accuracy. The Cave Troll coughs in agony and, dropping its club, staggers back, its massive meaty hands clawing at its thick throat. Abruptly it sits down and rolls about the floor of the cavern, wracked with pain, shrieking and wailing, eyeing you fearfully. It seems basically uninjured, simply in great pain. At the sight of the biggest among them incapacitated by a single blow, the other two back away from you. Smiling to yourself at their bullying, cowardly nature you turn your back on them and move on down the tunnel. Turn to **162**.

Your cat's claws let you climb the difficult north-west face of the peak, but to your dismay the monster follows. Then you hear the sound of a rockfall below and look down to see the monster tumbling and bouncing a thousand feet down an almost sheer face. At last the threat is lifted and you begin the descent, only to see the Golem clambering up towards you once more. There is only one narrow route if you wish to climb on (turn to **85**). If not, you may use the time gained by the Golem's fall to climb sideways and then down the north-eastern face (turn to **74**).

Using your power of mind over matter, you force yourself to ignore the threat that seems about to confront you and relax utterly. The root has freed your mind from the ties of belief which bind it to your body and your spirit flies free. You feel yourself floating gently upwards and below you can see Glaivas and the top of your own head, but Glaivas cannot see you. He starts as a dark shape begins to take the place of the swirling leaves, but your spirit is borne away suddenly by a gust of ethereal wind. In sudden panic you realise that you can hardly help yourself here on the spirit plane but you dimly sense pathways stretching through the ether. The dark shape looms behind you. The beast, whatever it is, has managed to follow you onto the spirit plane. The wind whirls you towards a parting of ways and something tells you that the right-hand path leads towards the gates of Heaven, whilst the left leads towards the Elysian Fields. You struggle to take one of the paths. Will you take the right path (turn to **295**) or the left (turn to **302**)?

You try to twist aside, but the dagger slides across your ribs, opening a deep wound and causing you to release your hold on Aiguchi and roll away from him. Lose 4 Endurance. If you are still alive, as you rise painfully to your feet, Aiguchi also rises, choking and gasping, his face locked in a grimace of pain. 'Impressive, ninja,' he grates between gritted teeth.

'You managed that well, but not well enough, for I am a Master of Weapons.' He picks up his curve-bladed spear and then executes a mind-boggling series of movements, as if he were fighting several opponents at once. The naginata is almost a blur as he thrusts and parries, performing a complex but deadly dance. You can see that he is very, very fast, but is he as fast as you? Then he begins to edge towards you, crab-like, the tip of his spear always pointed, unerringly, at your throat. You circle each other. Suddenly he hops and thrusts the spear at your belly with great speed, but you sweep it aside with your arm. For a brief moment you are inside the reach of the naginata. If you have the skill of Yubi-Jutsu, you realise he is too quick for you to use a precision nerve-strike, and you will have to slow him down first. Will you try the Leaping Tiger kick (turn to **56**), the Teeth of the Tiger throw (turn to **22**), a Tiger's Paw chop (turn to **38**) or wait for a suitable moment and, using Inner Force, attempt to snap Aiguchi's naginata (turn to **10**)?

154

Softly you speak a word of greeting. The girl freezes, then looks around wildly. She still cannot see you in the pitch darkness, but she shuffles away from you on her haunches. You speak gently to her once more and she demands to know, in a quavering but suspicious voice, who you are. Will you tell her the truth (turn to **174**) or say that you are temple guards at the Purple Cathedral to Death in the City of the Runes of Doom (turn to **185**)?

155

You can sense Doré relaxing behind you and you know you have said the right thing. He tells you something of himself as you journey together. He is indeed a fanatic. He has devoted his entire life to the persecution of evil and he has only those possessions which he needs to realise his goal, while the rest of his spoils he gives to the poor. His god is Rocheval, Prince of Knights Errant, wielder of the Holy of Holies. Legend has it that Rocheval was once a Paladin, a mortal who won the favour of Eo whilst campaigning in the

Abyss. So heroic and pure was he that he became a god, an enduring example to those who fight evil and chaos. He does not say so but you guess that Doré's dream is to take his own place in the Garden of the Gods. You become well-rested on the journey and Doré's hands have the magical touch of healing. You may restore any points of lost Endurance. Turn to **213**.

156

You must try to hit it harder than you have ever hit before. Deduct one point from your Inner Force.

FIEND FROM THE PIT
Defence against Cobra Strike punch: 10
Endurance: —
Damage: 2 Dice

If your blow strikes home forcefully, turn to **86**. If you failed you must try to block its ramming horn-spiking attack. Your Defence is 6. If you survive, will you use a Winged Horse kick (turn to **163**), a Dragon's Tail throw (turn to **178**), punch again (return to the top of this paragraph) or use the skill of Yubi-Jutsu if you have it (turn to **93**), or flee, leaving Glaivas on his own (turn to **201**)? You may only attempt a punch or kick if you have Inner Force left.

157

Your keen senses, honed to an almost superhuman degree of awareness, enable you to pick out the fine silvery thread of a trip-wire across your path. Had you walked into it, a viciously spiked wooden club would have sprung up from the ground where it was hidden under rotten leaves, and into your chest. Carefully, so as to avoid setting off the trap and thereby giving away your position, you skirt the area and come to the edge of the wood. Ahead, gently rolling ground carpeted in long grass leads to a pile of chalky rocks and boulders lining the rim of Hunter's Quarry. Will you head out to examine the Quarry – perhaps you can hide there (turn to **204**), or stay where you are and wait (turn to **190**)?

158

You chop with the side of your hand at one of the seams of flesh from which sickly-sweet ooze is still running, trying to split it asunder. You may add 3 to the damage done if you succeed.

GOLEM OF FLESH
Defence against Tiger's Paw chop: 4
Endurance: 25
Damage: 2 Dice

If you win, turn to **211**. Otherwise you feel your muscles going heavy with the prolonged effort. Your Defence against the hammering fists of the Golem is 7. If you survive will you use the Tiger's Paw chop again (return to the top of this paragraph), the Winged Horse kick (turn to **139**), or the Leaping Tiger kick (turn to **149**)?

159

Golspiel says that he thinks your plan is a good one. You are about to ask him where his mercenaries will attack but he tells you he is due to meet one of the Usurper's captains. If you have the skill of Shin-Ren, turn to **403**. If not, Golspiel concludes saying he will support you as far as he can. He gives you a Jade Lotus blossom as a token. Note the Jade Lotus on your Character Sheet. You bow and take your leave.

If you wish to approach another faction with whom you have not yet spoken, will it be the Swordswomen of Dama, Shieldmaiden of the Gods (turn to **296**), the priesthood of the Temple to Time (turn to **394**) or the rabble of the city (turn to **68**)? If you feel you have the support you need, you make your final preparations to assassinate the Usurper (turn to **9**).

160

'You do not look like a worshipper of the Great Redeemer. Surely you are an assassin?' The voice sounds like that of a young man. The language is the common tongue but the accent is like none you have ever heard. Will you say that you are a ninja from the Island of Tranquil Dreams (turn to **137**) or say that you kill only evil people and never without a cause (turn to **119**)?

161

At prayer in the small chapel you bare your soul to Kwon the Redeemer and pray for his guidance. After a while you sense that he is with you and your spirit is uplifted – you regain up to 3 points of Inner Force, if you have used any. Your prayer for guidance brings one cryptic message: 'Trust your heart.'

After the service you consult once more with the High Grandmaster. In the cold light of day he is racked with doubt, he fears that you may bring disaster to the Temple but he says that he will still support you and he gives you a map of the city.

He asks you to come and go in disguise, to which you gladly agree. You tell him that you intend to go among the people to learn their mood and to find out if it is possible to spark off a successful revolution and this calms him. You assume the disguise of a bond-serf: homespun breeches and jacket. At dusk you walk past the two broken bodies on their wheels and head back into the city itself in search of one of the three largest inns. Which will you visit first, the Cleansing Flame (turn to **105**), the Hostel from the Edge (turn to **78**), or the River of Beasts (turn to **62**)?

162

Relighting your torch you follow the tunnel for some time, padding silently through the darkness. It opens into a well-crafted square room, with walls of dressed stone. In the wall opposite stands an oak door, with leather panels studded with brass hooks. The right hand wall is smooth and flat, save for the faint outline of a door. In the middle of this outline is a small depression about the size of a coin. Examining it carefully you can make out a heraldic pattern carved into the stone. It is a hippogriff, part of the coat of arms of your own family. If you have played Book 2: *ASSASSIN!* and have a Brass Signet Ring, turn to **180**. If you have not, turn to **188**.

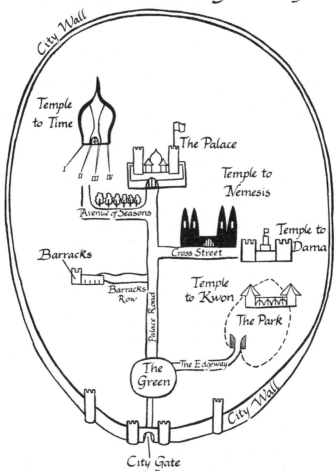

THE MAJOR TEMPLES OF IRSMUNCAST NIGH EDGE

City Wall

Temple to Time

The Palace

Temple to Nemesis

Avenue of Seasons

Temple to Dama

Barracks

Cross Street

Temple to Kwon

Barracks Row

Palace Road

The Park

The Green

The Edgeway

City Wall

City Gate

You must try to kick the Fiend harder than you have ever kicked before. Deduct one point from your Inner Force.

FIEND FROM THE PIT
Defence against Winged Horse kick: 11
Endurance: —
Damage: 2 Dice

If your blow strikes home forcefully, turn to **86**. If you failed you must try to block the powerful swipe of its horn-tipped arm as it tries to drive it deep into your head. Your Defence is 6. If you survive will you use a Cobra Strike punch (turn to **156**), a Dragon's Tail throw (turn to **178**), kick again (return to the top of this paragraph) or use the skill of Yubi-Jutsu if you have it (turn to **93**), or will you flee, leaving Glaivas on his own (turn to **201**)? You may only attempt a punch or kick if you have Inner Force left.

Stealthily, unheard and unseen, you make your way to the Fatestones. Gingerly you cross them and sprint away. You are putting distance between you and the Ring of Vasch-Ro when a strange chill takes hold and a wave of nausea washes over you for a second. You have been cursed by Fate because you quit the Ring of Vasch-Ro leaving the duel unfinished, and she has turned her back on you. You will fail the next three Fate Rolls. Note this down on your Character Sheet. Dejectedly you press on towards Irsmuncast nigh Edge. Turn to **416**.

165

As you join battle again, you realise that the Leaping Tiger kick requires a great deal of energy. Lose 2 Endurance as your limbs grow weary, but not if your Endurance is already at 2 or less.

GOLEM OF FLESH
Defence against Leaping Tiger kick: 5
Endurance: 25
Damage: 2 Dice

If you win, turn to **228**. Otherwise your Defence against the relentless pounding of the Golem's fists is 7. If you survive will you use the Leaping Tiger kick again (return to the top of this paragraph), the Winged Horse kick (turn to **191**) or the Tiger's Paw chop (turn to **179**)?

166

You run on, across the flat fields, towards a ring of low hills which mark the edge of the wilderness beyond. As you enter the basin between the hills a great column of fire reaches forty feet towards the sky before you. The glare shows a sight which chills you with fear. Atop each of the hills which encircle you stand two Spectral Knights. You are surrounded by the Spectral Company. Before you is a well and behind it stands Ganarre, eldritch brother of the Fleshless King. They begin to chant, drawing power from the shrine that was built many millennia ago, below the well. All will to resist leaves you and the Spectral Company close slowly in, to deprive you of life with their icy touch.

167

The root tastes bitter but its juices have an immediate effect, seeming to muddy your thoughts. You decide to try to find the Spirit Tiger on the spirit plane. You notice that a great bat-winged figure, the loathsome Fiend of your dreams, is taking shape on the spot where the leaves were swirling in the wind.

Will you try to project your mind into the spirit plane by

force of will (turn to **175**) or meditate and try to set your mind free from the shackles of your body (turn to **183**)?

168

Golspiel makes his displeasure evident and you try to think of a way of smoothing things over. If you have a Pouch of Rubies, a Potion of Healing or a magical Rune-Carved Dagger you may offer to bribe him (turn to **138**). Otherwise you must resign yourself to the fact that you have failed to enlist the support of the merchants.

Golspiel tells you he is due to meet one of the Usurper's captains. If you have the skill of Shin-Ren, turn to **403**. If not, Golspiel concludes saying he will not intervene but he gives you a Jade Lotus as a token of his esteem for your late father. Note it on your Character Sheet. You bow and take your leave.

If you wish to approach another faction with whom you have not yet spoken, will it be the Swordswomen of Dama, Shieldmaiden of the Gods (turn to **296**), the priesthood of the Temple to Time (turn to **394**) or the rabble of the city (turn to **68**)? If you feel you have the support you need, you make your final preparations to assassinate the Usurper (turn to **9**).

169

Doré reins in his horse. You dismount and he turns his charger saying, 'I have enjoyed our discussion but my conscience pulls me. There is much work left undone in the Rift. Farewell.'

With that he sets spur to his horse and is soon lost to sight. You continue on your way. Turn to **199**.

170

You have dealt with it severely and your last blow sends it staggering back gasping in pain. It drops its club and backs up, moaning and eyeing you fearfully. It doubles up and hugs itself, whimpering pathetically. At the sight of the largest amongst them cowering in agony, the other two back away, obviously not prepared to take you on. Smiling to yourself at their cowardly bullying nature, you turn your back on them and move on down the tunnel. Turn to **162**.

171

'Then die, black-garbed assassin!' shouts the figure, drawing the huge bastard sword from his back and charging you. You decide to dodge and use a Leaping Tiger kick to knock him from the saddle. The sword shines with a silver radiance. Turn to **262**.

172

The High Grandmaster tells you that the largest temples in the city are to Nemesis, Kwon, Dama the Shieldmaiden of the Gods, and Time. He says that what power still remains in the city, apart from that of the Usurper and the Temple to Nemesis, is divided into four groups. The Temple to Time is powerful for it also is not subject to a temple tax and its priests and their followers enjoy special privileges under the Usurper's rule. You ask why this is and the High Grandmaster tells you that according to the sages of Greyguilds, Time is the most powerful of all the gods. The Snowfather has more temples and worshippers dedicated to him than any other. 'Good and Evil mean nothing to Time, indeed it would take me a year to tell you what the worship of Time entails, but the Usurper does not see his priests as a threat, even though people are turning to Time to escape the heavy taxes. Nonetheless, the priests of Time are not allied to the Usurper.'

'Next in power are the merchants, led by Golspiel of the Silver Tongue. They have mercenaries at their beck and call and can afford to pay the Usurper's taxes. Merchants always know a great deal about the underworld and power struggles in any city.'

'Third comes the Temple to Dama, Shieldmaiden of the Gods. Under your father's rule they were the city watch and gateguards – they kept law and order. The followers of Dama are valiant fighters but they are outnumbered by the Usurper's army. '

'Lastly the rabble, the dispossessed, the bond-slaves and

any who have the Usurper to thank for their wretched plight. More than half the city, but without a leader to unite them, they are nothing. With a leader...' The Grandmaster spreads his hands.

You thank him and he invites you to pray with him on the morrow. Until then you will sleep, safe perhaps, for this one night. Turn to **161**.

173

You move forward as silently as possible, to within ten feet of him, hoping he will not hear you or turn around. Make a Fate Roll. If Fate smiles on you, turn to **376**. If Fate turns her back on you, turn to **389**.

174

You tell the slave girl that you are journeying to your homeland in the Manmarch and that you have chosen to pass through this dangerous region to trick your many enemies who wish you dead. Glaivas says merely that he is a Ranger who is helping his friend. She creeps closer to see you more clearly and when you show no sign of wishing to do her harm she volunteers her name, Grizell. She tells you that she is an orphan, her sisters have been taken away by the Priests of Death, for sacrifice, and she pleads with you to take her with you. There is utter desperation in her frail voice and you realise you are her only hope, for tomorrow the orcish overseers will catch her. You look at Glaivas, but he looks away, offering no help. Will you take Grizell with you (turn to **193**) or dig the Ranger in the ribs and motion that you wish to leave (turn to **206**)?

175

You still your wildly beating heart and try to project your mind onto the spirit plane, but it stays firmly rooted within your body and as you watch the Fiend becomes real flesh and blood before you. Suddenly there is a great banshee wail that torments your ears. 'Aiee, how it pains me to journey to this plane of life.' The Fiend's voice curdles your blood and everything seems to speed up suddenly, but your own movements become agonizingly ponderous as the Fiend launches itself into the air, its wings casting a pall of shadow blacker than night, its great club-horned arms ready to smash your body to a wet pulp. The Fiend's magic has slowed your movements. You don't think that a shuriken would harm it; will you step back and say the Ninja's Covenant, Ninja No Chigiri (turn to **226**), try a Leaping Tiger kick (turn to **234**), duck behind a tree and hope the spell will wear off (turn to **243**) or if you are skilled with Poison Needles you may wish to use one (turn to **255**).

176

Golspiel seems pleased and he inquires a little about your plans. Will you tell him you intend to enter the dungeons and then kill the Usurper (turn to **159**) or tell him nothing but ask what he will do to help (turn to **130**)?

177

The side of your hand, hardened by years of training, cracks the shaft of the naginata. It snaps like a twig with a sharp report under the awesome power of your Inner Force. Aiguchi is left holding a broken shaft of wood in his hand and he gapes in astonishment at what you have done. 'Quite remarkable, ninja,' he says. Then he smiles and continues, 'But I am a Master of Weapons,' and he reaches inside his scarlet jacket and pulls out a nunchaku – two batons linked by a short chain. He whirls this around his head and body, and from hand to hand, setting up a breathtaking pattern of blurs humming through the air. He stops suddenly, legs braced apart, left hand outstretched towards you, right hand holding part of the nunchaku, the other half of it tucked under his right arm. He smiles evilly at you and dives forward, somersaulting and whipping the nunchaku down at your head as he comes up. Your Defence is 8 as you try to intercept it with your iron sleeves. If it hits you it will do 1 Die + 1 damage. If you still live will you attack with the Whirlpool throw (turn to **46**), the Winged Horse kick (turn to **89**) or the Cobra Strike punch (turn to **303**)?

You slide towards the great hooves in a flurry of leaves but the enormous wings crack once more against the night and the Fiend rises above you, then lashes out with its hooves. Your Defence against the stamping hooves is 5. If it hits you, it will do 2 Dice + 1 damage. If you survive this attack you manage to regain your feet, but the Fiend is attacking again.

If you have the skill of Yubi-Jutsu, Nerve-Striking, and wish to use it, turn to **93**. If not will you use a Winged Horse kick (turn to **163**) or a Cobra Strike punch (turn to **156**), or will you flee, leaving Glaivas on his own (turn to **201**)? You may only attempt a punch or kick if you have Inner Force left.

Conserving as much energy as you can, you chop at the seams in the monster's flesh. You may add 2 to any damage you do using this attack.

GOLEM OF FLESH
Defence against Tiger's Paw chop: 4
Endurance: 25
Damage: 2 Dice

If you win, turn to **228**. Otherwise the rapidly hammering fists bludgeon at you and your Defence is 8. If you survive, will you use the Tiger's Paw chop again (return to the top of this paragraph), the Winged Horse kick (turn to **191**) or the Leaping Tiger kick (turn to **165**)?

With a flash of insight, you remember that the Brass Signet Ring also depicts a hippogriff and that it is just the right size to fit into the depression. You take it out and place it into the hole. It fits perfectly. Suddenly there is a loud click and a grinding sound and the slab in front of you begins to sink into the ground. Bright light floods out from the room beyond. Walking through the secret entrance, you find yourself in a large circular chamber. Immediately before you on the ground is a stone slab, the resting place of a long-dead

Lord of Irsmuncast. In the centre of the room stands a marble plinth surrounded by a ring of flames. Upon the plinth rests a thin gold circlet. It is adorned with a single sparkling ruby that glitters in the light. This must be the item you were told would be of use against the Usurper.

You cannot discern what the flames are feeding off – indeed there is something very odd about the fire. It gives off a bright white light and the flames flicker and burn about an inch off the ground. The flames are a coppery yellow and seem insubstantial in some way. Stepping closer you quickly pass your hand through the flame. An agonizing pain fills your soul for an instant, burning at the core of your being. You realise that these are not physical flames but ethereal flames and that they would not leave your clothes and skin charred and blackened but your very soul itself.

Do you have a bottle containing Waters of Protection from Ethereal Flame? If you do, turn to **225**. If you do not, turn to **212**.

181

The High Grandmaster is an old man. His watery eyes hold wisdom but he has lost the strength of his body. You show him your father's seal, the hippogriff on the chequerboard, and the birthmark. He hails you as a deliverer from the evil tyranny of the Usurper – it is plain that he feels his own weakness and inability to oppose the despot keenly. You talk far into the night and he tells you how things stand in the city of Irsmuncast nigh Edge.

Since your father the Loremaster's death, the cruel Usurper has tyrannised the people, killing all who oppose him and grinding the spirit of the peasants underfoot. The farmers have had their land taken away from them and now they are bond-slaves, tied to the land, forced to give a half of everything they grow to feed the Usurper's army of Orcs and Halvorcs. To be married, couples must gain a permit from the Usurper's Lord Steward. Worshippers of Avatar and Kwon are often refused this and so cannot have legitimate children. Bastards can never inherit. Crippling taxes have been imposed on almost all, but of course those who worship

Nemesis are excluded. This means that many are forced to renounce their belief and turn to evil if they are to be anything but miserably poor.

The priests of Nemesis and the Usurper's army rule with naked swords but still they cannot close the opposing temples. 'The temple tax is high', says the Grandmaster. 'We cannot pay our due, but even the Usurper cannot turn us out. We have no power but that over people's minds.'

You explain that you have come to take your rightful throne and he pledges the support of the Temple, but says that it will not be enough to kill the tyrant. There must be a revolution to overturn the army and the priests of Nemesis. The martial arts tradition of this Temple to Kwon is not strong so you will have to seek support for the revolution elsewhere before you slay the Usurper.

Turn to **172**.

182

Suddenly your foot makes contact with a thin wire stretched across your path. There is a loud click. Do you have the skill of Acrobatics? If you do, turn to **233**. If not, turn to **239**.

183

Using your power of mind over matter you force yourself to ignore the Fiend and relax utterly. The root has freed your mind from the ties of belief which bind it to your body and your spirit flies free. You feel yourself floating gently upwards and below you can see Glaivas and the top of your own head, but Glaivas cannot see you. The Fiend has become real flesh and blood and there is a great banshee wail: 'Aiee, how it pains me to journey to this plane of life.'

The Fiend's voice curdles your blood but you feel strangely detached. Glaivas seems to slow down as if suddenly stricken with age as the monster launches itself into the air, its wings casting a pall of shadow blacker than the night, its great club-horned arms ready to smash your motionless body to a wet pulp.

Suddenly the ethereal wind rushes your spirit far away but you feel the pull of your body as it suffers the first attack of the Fiend. You lose 8 Endurance as the horns smash your ribcage. Regardless of your Endurance remaining, even if it is 0 or less, turn to **344**.

184

When you tell the High Grandmaster that you wish to enlist the support of the merchants he says that he has no dealings with them but that, if you go now, you will find their spokesman, Golspiel of the Silver Tongue, in the spice emporium on Low End Road near the Green. He adds that the merchants keep a large number of mercenary soldiers in their pay.

You head towards the Green to make your inquiries and are escorted thence by two evil-looking mercenaries in purple livery. Golspiel has just completed the auction of some jewellery when you find him in his emporium which is a great purple pavilion furnished with exotica from far away lands. His eyes are like small shining currants in a face that shudders every time he moves. His fat jowls hang down like dewlaps and his hands look like balloons. He smiles and asks in a smooth persuasive voice what your business is. You tell him straight away who you are, showing him your father's hippogriff and chequerboard seal and your birthmark. He is sceptical at first, but something about you convinces him that your father was indeed the Loremaster. Then you tell him that you are fated to overthrow the Usurper and become Overlord in his place, asking for Golspiel's support in the revolution. The merchant gives nothing away but he begins to persuade you that you must lift all taxes on the traders when you are Overlord and suggests that all those desiring to become merchants should apply to him for a certificate allowing them to trade. Will you tell him that you will give these concessions in return for his support (turn to **176**)? Or say that you will give these things thought but it is too soon to make such promises (turn to **168**)?

185

'No! No!' the slave girl shrieks piercingly at the top of her voice, her cry shattering the quiet of the night. She is already backing out from under the awning and you realise that she thinks you have come to take her for sacrifice on the altar of the Purple Cathedral. Glaivas pulls you back out from under your side of the awning and sets off at a run. A myriad flickering orange lights pierce the darkness all around you. The slave-guards are taking up the hunt and the Slave Fields are alive with dancing orange torches, like fireflies, which threaten to hem you in. You are forced to run east to try to escape. At last you are leaving the bobbing torches behind but you are becoming tired. Turn to **166**.

186

The tramp takes you to the Green and then points to the way east before hobbling away as you thank him. Turn to **269**.

187

Glaivas' sword is like a rod of red ruin as he meets the grotesque Halvorcs in combat. Four of them cluster around you, jabbing with their spears. For each attack you are forced to make, you stand a chance of being wounded. You decide to use kicks to batter them senseless.

FOUR HALVORCS
Defence against kick: 5
Endurance (per Halvorc): 9
Damage: 1 Die

Every time you attack, you must make a Fate Roll, but use only one die. If you score 1 or 2 on one die, you have been hit. You are unable to block. If you win, turn to **95**.

188

Will you examine the wall to see if you can open what seems to be a secret door (turn to **194**) or will you go through the brass-studded oak door (turn to **207**)?

189

The Throne Room is silent. No trace of Astaroth remains. The rose-crown lies wedged against the statue of Dama, but you leave it where it lies. There is yet much to do.

Outside the Throne Room the corridors are deserted. Your garrotte slices through the throat of an orcish guard on the landing and then you are climbing the eastern-most tower of the Palace. The top of the winding stair ends at the tower roof. The sky is blue above the battlements. The Usurper's flag, a stag with spiralling horns and a barbed tail, flutters in the breeze. A single pull on the rope draws it down below the battlements.

If you carry a Statuette of the Goddess Dama and a Coronation Day Coin, turn to **361**. If you obtained only the Statuette, turn to **100**. If you have the Coin only, turn to **370**. If you have neither of these tokens, turn to **378**.

190
After a while you notice a flicker of movement amongst the rocks at the edge of the Quarry. It must be Aiguchi! You decide to try and crawl stealthily through the long grass and creep up behind Aiguchi's position. Make a Fate Roll. If Fate smiles on you, turn to **217**. If Fate turns her back on you, turn to **223**.

191
Using kicks takes more energy than punching and you are exhausted from battle and flight. Lose 1 Endurance for the effort you put into the Winged Horse kick, but not if your Endurance is already at 1.

GOLEM OF FLESH
Defence against Winged Horse kick: 5
Endurance: 25
Damage: 2 Dice

If you win, turn to **228**. Otherwise the hammer blows of its fists drive towards you again and your Defence is 7. If you survive, will you use the Winged Horse kick again (return to the top of this paragraph), the Leaping Tiger kick (turn to **165**) or the Tiger's Paw chop (turn to **179**)?

As you put the mandrake root into your mouth, the Fiend becomes real flesh and blood before you and lets forth a great banshee wail that torments your ears, 'Aiee, how it pains me to journey to this plane of life.'

The Fiend's voice curdles your blood and everything seems to speed up suddenly, but your own movements become agonizingly ponderous as the Fiend launches itself into the air, its wings casting a pall of shadow blacker than night, its great clubbed arms ready to smash your body to a wet pulp. The root has an immediate effect, muddying your thoughts.

You can try to enter the spirit plane to look for the Spirit Tiger (turn to **288**), step back and say the Ninja's Covenant, Ninja No Chigiri (turn to **226**), try a Leaping Tiger kick (turn to **234**), duck behind a tree and hope the spell will wear off (turn to **243**) or if you are skilled with Poison Needles you may wish to use one (turn to **255**).

Glaivas groans quietly as you tell Grizell that you will save her. The surprise and hope in her voice make the risk seem worthwhile. Grizell huddles close to you, her bony body hard against your firm muscles. She takes a locket from its place of concealment in her hair and hands it to you, saying that an old, old woman gave it to her for protection in the slave train. It is blue porcelain, in the shape of a heart, and it opens up to reveal a wispy lock of golden hair.

'It is the forelock of a girl who never told a lie in her whole life. She was a saint. Keep it, I don't need it now that I have you to protect me. Why is your face all covered up?'

You thank her for the locket and stow it away safely. Note the Saint's Locket on your Character Sheet.

'Come, we must leave this place,' you say, and Grizell follows you both out from under the awning.

'We had better turn north, away from the city,' says Glaivas.

Turn to **215**.

194

You run your hands up and down the edges of the door-like slab in the wall, searching for a way to open it if possible. If you have the skill of Picking Locks, Detecting and Disarming Traps, turn to **290**. If not, turn to **256**.

195

A spark falls onto the bone dry robes and begins to smoulder as it catches fire. It crackles and roars into life. The corpse is suddenly engulfed in flame and its hands open reflexively, releasing you. You stagger back, coughing and retching, massaging your bruised throat as you watch the corpse burn. It is consumed in flame and soon there is nothing left but ash. Note down the Rune-Carved Dagger on your Character Sheet. After you have rested you decide to go down the tunnel and leave this place of horror. Turn to **367**.

196

One of the Halvorcs hurls his spear at you, but you knock it aside with ease. Turn to **187**.

197

At your refusal to run, Glaivas curses and returns to the battle. Glaivas' sword seems to do no damage to the Fiend and it ignores him, casting him aside bodily like a toy whenever he comes between you. The Fiend comes for you, ungainly on its cloven-hooved feet but redolent of great power, its wings cracking against the night air. Will you use the Dragon's Tail throw (turn to **178**), a Winged Horse kick (turn to **163**), a Cobra Strike punch (turn to **156**) or the skill of Yubi-Jutsu if you have it (turn to **93**), or will you flee leaving Glaivas to fight the Fiend on his own (turn to **201**)?

198

You become dimly aware of shouting and a clash of arms that has been echoing from somewhere in the Palace. The doors to the Throne Room burst open and Doré le Jeune enters with a rattle of armour. He has fought his way through the guards to the Throne Room alone. 'I smelt evil.

We meet again Scourge, Astaroth! I am honoured but your sojourn on Orb is at an end.' With that he rushes to the attack, his holy sword cutting glittering arcs through the air as he engages Astaroth and the Devils of Twilight together. You must fight Scourge. Once again you decide to use kicks against him as he is too tall for punches really to affect him.

SCOURGE THE CENTAUR DEVIL
Defence against Leaping Tiger kick: 7
Defence against Kwon's Flail: 5
Damage: 2 Dice + 2
Endurance: 22

Note that any injuries you previously inflicted on Scourge still apply. Your blows affect Scourge as if he were a normal beast, while he is not in hell, but Inner Force does not affect him. The Saint's Locket and the Ruby Circlet will protect you against Scourge as they did against Astaroth, as the Centaur Devil rears and smashes down his iron hooves to stave in your skull. Your Defence as you try to leap aside is 7, or 8 if you have the skill of Acrobatics. If Scourge is still attacking, you must kick him again.

    If you win, Scourge disappears, banished to the spirit plane, and Astaroth alone of the devils remains. Doré le Jeune is wounded and too exhausted to carry on. You must fight Astaroth again, but he has been weakened by the Paladin's attentions and magical blade. You choose to use the Iron Fist punch.

ASTAROTH
Defence against Iron Fist punch: 8
Endurance: 6
Damage: 3 Dice

Special conditions no longer apply when striking him. When defending yourself, the Saint's Locket and the Ruby Circlet protect as before. If you win, turn to **388**. If Astaroth still fights on, you try to avoid his champing jaws, and your Defence is 8. If you survive you punch again.

Your journey to the city of Irsmuncast lasts several days and passes without incident. You rest and recuperate on the way: you may restore any points of lost Endurance. At last the walls of Irsmuncast show blue on the horizon. Turn to **236.**

As quick as lightning you hurl the Shuriken with deadly accuracy. It strikes the Werewolf in the chest. Its reaction is instantaneous. It rears up on its hind legs howling in agony and clawing at the wound desperately. The Shuriken seems to be burning into it, but the creature manages to claw the throwing star out of its chest to be lost somewhere amid the stones. Cross it off your Character Sheet and note that the Werewolf has lost 7 from its Endurance of 14.

If you have reduced it to 0 Endurance, it slowly collapses to the ground: turn to **57.** Otherwise, you take this opportunity to close for another attack. Will you try an Iron Fist punch (turn to **67**), a Forked Lightning kick (turn to **219**) or a Teeth of the Tiger throw (turn to **364**)?

As you sprint through the trees you can hear Glaivas's battle-cry, then nothing. You run on, hoping to put as much distance as you can between yourself and them, but you are not as used to finding your way in an unknown forest at night as Glaivas. At last you come out into a wide clearing lit by the moon and pull up short before what looks like an ancient tomb. You decipher some of the words carved on the stone: you have come to the Crypts of Arkadan.

Remembering the Ranger's words, you turn to leave, but you cannot. You are rooted to the spot. Looking around you notice a pile of dust nearby and then you realise that the stone at its edge is part of a man's rotting skull. Then the Fiend is above you, shutting out the moon with its wings. 'My task is completed,' it cries and then melts away before your eyes.

You will never move again.

'What are you? You have the look of an assassin.'

Will you reply by attacking with a throwing star (turn to **274**), say that you are called by some Avenger and that you worship Kwon the Redeemer (turn to **160**), say your name is Malvolio and that you worship Nemesis, Lord of the Cleansing Fire (turn to **141**) or say that you are called Temperance by those who know you well and that you worship Innoka, the Innocent Friend to All (turn to **129**)?

You try to block the first of the spears, but it pierces your thigh, knocking you back as the rest are hurled at you. You are transfixed, two spears passing through your body and into the hedge. The Halvorcs decide to finish you with their whips, but mercifully death takes you fast.

You move out towards the quarry looking around you carefully.

Just as you take your eyes off the quarry, the air is filled with a high-pitched whine. Looking back you see Aiguchi silhouetted against the stones. You realise he is using Humming Bulb arrows that whistle in the air. Do you have the skill of Arrow Cutting? If you do, turn to **63**. If you do not, turn to **92**.

You tell the tramp that you are from the Island of Tranquil Dreams but he says he has never heard of it and walks on, turning left after a hundred yards. He leads you through an archway into a small cobbled square and then throws himself to the floor and whistles. If you have the skill of Acrobatics, turn to **24**. If not, you find yourself surrounded by soldiers from the Usurper's army. The tramp has led you into one of their barracks. You are overpowered after a long struggle, bound and taken to the Palace. If you are skilled in Escapology, turn to **8**. Otherwise you suffer a grisly fate. When your birthmark is discovered the Usurper orders you to be put to the ultimate torture, but you bite off your own tongue and bleed to death, cheating him of his pleasure.

206

You nudge Glaivas and he nods, then, leaning forwards, he kindles a light with his flint and tinder, looking at the girl's face. It is thin and drawn, but pretty. The light goes out and the girl cannot see at all in the pitch darkness until her eyes adapt again. She gropes towards you but you are gone without a sound, unseen. Glaivas sighs heavily, then says, 'Should we turn north, towards the mountains?' Will you turn north (turn to **123**) or continue east (turn to **166**)?

207

You approach the door and listen at it but no sounds come to you from the other side. You put your hand on the door-handle and turn it experimentally. It is unlocked and you swing it open and step into a richly furnished room, the walls of which are lined with shelves packed with scrolls and books. Behind a large ornately carved desk sits a strange figure, looking up in surprise as you come in with eyes that are completely white, save for the pupils, two pin-points of blackness. Its face is hideous, it is totally bald, the skin a pale blotchy colour. Below the flat nostrils of its boneless nose, five tentacles each about a foot in length writhe horribly. Just below these is the mouth, small and circular with sharp pointed teeth. It wears purple robes edged with gold and there is an ancient tome open on the desk in front of it. Its hands end in three long, thin tentacles, in place of fingers. You recognise it from ancient books and drawings as an Old One, a race of creatures that inhabit the depth of the Rift. Utterly evil and said to be schemers and ultimate leaders, other than the gods, of much that is evil on Orb.

The Old One stands slowly and speaks in a sibilant whispering voice, 'This is indeed an unexpected pleasure! Welcome! Welcome! You must be Avenger, the, er, "rightful" heir to the throne of Irsmuncast. I have heard a lot about you, ninja. The Usurper and I hoped you would not get this far, but it appears you are more resourceful than we had

imagined. Still it does mean the pleasure of your annihilation shall be all mine.'

Suddenly your mind is assailed by a blast of mental energy and you realise the Old One is launching a psychic attack against you. You feel your will literally beginning to shred under the awesome power of the creature's mind. You find yourself virtually unable to move, your mind locked in a deadly battle of wills. Do you have any Inner Force left? If you do, turn to **323**. If not, turn to **335**.

208

Gwyneth nods and says that you can count on the support of the Temple to Dama and two thousand trained sword-arms. You tell her that you will kill the Usurper yourself, then lower his flag on the Palace which will be the signal for her to attack the Usurper's soldiers. You spend some time talking battle tactics. The Usurper has five thousand men and Orcs but not all would remain loyal. She is clearly a gifted general and she despises the Usurper with all her heart. You leave the Temple in good spirits fingering a small Statuette of the Goddess Dama which she has given you as a token of her support. Note it on your Character Sheet.

You can return to the Temple to Kwon and ask the Grandmaster to help you approach a faction whom you have not yet spoken with for support, either the priesthood of the Temple to Time (turn to **394**) or the merchants in their emporia (turn to **184**), or try to kindle the rabble (turn to **68**). Or if you feel you have the support you need, make your final preparations to assassinate the Usurper (turn to **9**).

209

Glaivas leads you into a part of the forest where the trees grow close together and your excellent night vision is tested to the limit. The Fiend's wings cannot help it here, there is no room for them to be spread, but you can hear its banshee howl above the trees. It is somehow tracking you and the howl curdles your blood. You begin to feel hot, sweat breaks out all over you; it is the Fiend's magic. Glaivas says, 'I'm burning, now is the time to ask for the Spirit Tiger's aid.' If you have already eaten the mandrake root turn to **132**. If not, you eat the mandrake root and straight away your thoughts become muddied. Will you try to force your mind onto the spirit plane through willpower (turn to **147**) or meditate and relax to try to set your mind free of the shackles of your body (turn to **277**)?

210

Desperately you fumble for your flint and tinder as its grip tightens even further. Your lungs begin to burn with agony. You send sparks flying onto its dry robes. Make a Fate Roll. If Fate smiles on you, turn to **195**. If Fate turns her back on you, then the clothes do not catch fire and you lose 3 Endurance as you are slowly strangled. If you are still alive you can try to set it alight again (return to the top of this paragraph), plunge the dagger back into its chest (turn to **398**) or try to chop its hand away from your throat with a Tiger's Paw chop (turn to **382**).

211

This time your blow has pole-axed the Golem which crashes to the dewy grass. Once again it disappears and you are breathing heavily now. You wait in an agony of suspense. Something is moving in the mist. The Golem sways towards you once more, the cracked voice sending a thrill of fear through you as it repeats the words, 'My name is Everyman and I am Legion.' How many times must you give battle to this monster, you wonder. You decide to flee, you need to recover and think. Turn to **230**.

212

Will you leave the chamber and go through the brass-studded oak door (turn to **207**) or try to dash through the flames and grab the circlet (turn to **235**)?

213

After several days, the walls of Irsmuncast show blue on the horizon. When you arrive, Doré says, 'I must turn back to the Rift, but I will return. Farewell, may you never stray from the straight and narrow path that leads to the Seven Heavens.' You dismount and wave farewell. Turn to **236**.

214

Gwyneth's face is stern as she says, 'The Loremaster's blood does not run true in his child. You would have me plunge the city into the chaos of revolution for the sake of a promise you cannot keep and I do not want. Begone and do not enter this holy temple of Law again.' You can see that no argument you make will sway her, so you resign yourself to a revolution without the help of the swordswomen.

You can return to the Temple to Kwon and ask the Grandmaster to help you approach a faction whom you have not yet spoken with for support, either the priesthood of the Temple to Time (turn to **394**) or the merchants in their emporia (turn to **184**), or try to kindle the rabble (turn to **68**). Or if you feel you have the support you need, make your final preparations to assassinate the Usurper (turn to **9**).

215

You run for many miles towards the mountains which tower blackly above you, carrying Grizell when she can run no further. She is nothing but a sack of bones, weighing less than a corn stack. Your acute sense of hearing picks up the sound of distant hoofbeats and you have a premonition of doom. Grizell wails in fear. You tell Glaivas that there are four horses approaching and he says, 'They have found us. We must make a stand.' Grizell climbs down from your back and you climb quickly towards a narrow canyon mouth, flanked by sheer cliffs, and wait. Turn to **268**.

216

The tramp's face is lined and dirty and he is lame in one leg. He thrusts your coin into a pocket in his tattered breeches and asks obsequiously if he can show you to an inn where you may find a bed for the night. Will you ask him to take you to the Temple to Kwon and offer him more gold (turn to **377**), say that you want a quiet inn for the night (turn to **343**) or thank him but go your own way (turn to **317**)?

217

Without a sound you inch your way around the Weaponmaster's position. Then you thread your way, still undetected, through the tumbled rocks beside the Quarry until Aiguchi is some twenty feet in front of you. He is crouched behind a large boulder, occasionally popping his head up to survey the ground ahead of him. Obviously he was hoping to pick you off with the bow he holds in his hands. Will you hurl a shuriken at him (turn to **415**)? If you have the skill of Poison Needles, you could try to spit a needle at him although it is at extreme range (turn to **148**). Otherwise, you can try to creep up silently behind him (turn to **173**).

218

Glaivas' sword buries itself into one of its wings whilst you drive a Leaping Tiger kick at its face. There is a faint noise like the Death-Knell of the great bell in the Iron-city of Dis deep in the Underworld. Note that you have heard a Death-Knell. Things seem to speed up all around and, for a moment, your own movements become agonisingly slow, then it passes and you duck beneath a scything of the Fiend's horn-tipped arm. To your dismay neither your kick nor the Ranger's sword seem even to have marked the Fiend's skin. Glaivas calls, 'There is nothing we can do to harm it. It cannot stay too long on this plane, follow me,' and with that he begins to run. Will you follow (turn to **209**) or stay to fight (turn to **197**)?

219

You whip your foot up twice in quick succession at the slavering jaws of your assailant as it tries to rake you with its taloned paws.

WEREWOLF
Defence against Forked Lightning kick: 7
Endurance: 14
Damage: 1 Die + 2

If you have killed it, turn to **57**. If it is still alive as your foot flies up to it for the second time, it tries to catch your leg and clamp its jaws around your ankle. Your Defence is 6. If you are still alive, will you kick again (return to the top of this paragraph), punch (turn to **67**) or throw (turn to **364**) the beast?

220

Gwyneth's face is stern as she says, 'The Loremaster's blood does not run true in his child. You would have me plunge the city into the chaos of revolution for the sake of a trifle. Begone and do not enter this holy temple of Law again.' You can see that no argument you make will sway her, so you resign yourself to a revolution without the help of the swordswomen.

You can return to the Temple to Kwon and ask the Grandmaster to help you approach a faction whom you have not yet spoken with for support, either the priesthood of the Temple to Time (turn to **394**) or the merchants in their emporia (turn to **184**), or try to kindle the rabble (turn to **68**). Or if you feel you have the support you need, make your final preparations to assassinate the Usurper (turn to **9**).

221

The tramp recognises you instantly as you walk into the crowded room. He is not a tramp at all but one of the Usurper's secret informers. He denounces you as a traitor and Halvorcs and Orcs rush towards you. You fight your way to the door to see it guarded by the Wolfen. One of them takes you from behind and after a fierce battle another rips out your throat with one swipe of his clawed paw.

222

You deftly catch the first of their spears and knock two more aside by their shafts. Several more have missed, thudding into the hedge. Only five of the Halvorcs still have spears with which to threaten you. You drop down into the corn and creep up on them, exploding into a flurry of violence in their midst. You have disarmed, killed or set to flight the Halvorcs within a matter of seconds – their bullwhips are ineffectual as weapons and you have lost only 2 Endurance.

If this is not itself enough to end your life, will you climb the Palisade and try to skirt the Walls of Shadow to the south (turn to **144**) or try to track down Glaivas once more (turn to **133**)?

223

You are crawling through the grass towards the Quarry when you hear a noise ahead of you. You raise your head just in time to see Aiguchi above you. With a cry of triumph he tries to pin you to the ground with his curve-bladed spear, the naginata.

You roll aside and leap to your feet, springing back away from him as the naginata sinks into the earth. 'Try and sneak up on me, eh, you ninja scum! I will make you pay for that.' He begins to edge towards you, crab-like, the tip of his spear always pointed, unerringly, at your throat. You circle each other. Suddenly he hops and thrusts the spear at your belly with great speed, but you sweep it aside with your arm. For a brief moment you are inside the reach of the naginata. If you have the skill of Yubi-Jutsu, you realise he is too quick for you to use a precision nerve-strike, and you will have to slow him down first. Will you try the Leaping Tiger kick (turn to **56**), the Teeth of the Tiger throw (turn to **22**), a Tiger's Paw chop (turn to **38**) or wait for a suitable moment and, using Inner Force, attempt to snap Aiguchi's naginata {turn to **10**)?

224

You fight as ever before whilst Glaivas' scroll seems to have banished one of his foes which turns to dust in moments. He has cast a Raise the Dead spell on the long undead Warlord. You spin and kick but the Spectre's cold touch draws the life force from you. You feel a chill in your heart and the will to resist leaves you. As Glaivas is forced back you become a shadow in the service of the Spectral Knight who has slain you.

225

You drink the contents of the bottle, hoping that its effects will enable you to pass through the flames unhurt (cross it off your Character Sheet). The liquid is virtually tasteless and you do not feel any different in any way, but you step towards the flames and, steeling yourself, jump through them towards the plinth. It is as if they did not exist and you breathe a sigh of relief as you pick up the golden circlet and place it on your head, under your hood. The circlet does not have any apparent effect in any way, but you know this must be the item you sought (note the Ruby Circlet on your Character Sheet). You leave the circular chamber and find yourself back at the brass-studded oak door. You have little choice but to go through it. Turn to **207**.

226

Saying the Ninja's Covenant steadies your resolve but does nothing to break the spell of ponderousness cast upon you by the Fiend's voice. It swoops down upon you and you dive aside, but too slowly, and one of its horny arms catches you a glancing blow. Turn to **396**.

227

The figure leans forward slightly in the saddle and speaks. 'Who are you and if you are not godless, which divine spirit holds your fealty?' He is asking which god you worship. Will you refuse to say anything (turn to **171**), say that you are called by some 'Avenger' and that you worship Kwon the Redeemer (turn to **160**), say your name is 'Malvolio' and you worship Nemesis, Lord of the Cleansing Fire (turn to **141**) or say that you are called 'Temperance' by those who know you well and that you worship Innoka, the Innocent Friend to All (turn to **129**)?

228

Once more the stricken Golem disappears. Your chest burns with the effort of dispatching it and you suck in lungfuls of air, waiting, tensely expectant to see if it will return. Nothing happens, you sigh deeply then catch your breath – its form is taking shape again before you and once again you hear the awful words, 'My name is Everyman and I am Legion.'

You back away, then turn to run as Everyman lopes relentlessly towards you. You run for several more miles until you are once more gasping for breath and still the Golem follows. If you wish to fight it again to find out if it has only one life left, turn to **259**. If you would like to try and enlist some divine aid by praying, turn to **348**. If you would like to head for the Mountains of Horn to see if it will fall to destruction, following you as you climb a peak, turn to **357**.

229

You leap back as Scourge's iron hooves throw up a shower of marble chips and your blood runs cold as you hear Astaroth and Scourge cry together, 'Hazarbol and Mazarbol, Devils of Twilight, come to us.' If you still have a Potion of Healing or Bag of Herbs you may use it now as two more horrendous forms appear before the throne (restore your Endurance to 20). Two hyenas as large as the gates of the Temple of the Rock, with eyes of liquid fire, stare at you balefully, tensing as if to spring. If you travelled to Irsmuncast on the piebald charger of a paladin, turn to **198**, as the Devils of Twilight begin to laugh so loudly that you can hardly think for terror. Otherwise you will have to think of something else as the odds against you are becoming impossibly high. If you have, and wish to use, a magical Rune-Carved Dagger, turn to **121**. If you wish to hurl your father's seal at his coat of arms and ask his spirit to aid you, turn to **90**. If you have a Statuette of the Goddess Dama and you wish to take it out and pray, turn to **75**.

230

As you lope away through the mist you can hear the Golem's heavy footfalls behind you. It is lumbering along at a run and you realise that it will not rest until it has killed you. In all likelihood it would follow you to the ends of Orb. Certainly, you realise it would be folly to trail this monstrosity behind you to Irsmuncast. With every step the monster takes it is liable to draw your enemies to you and you will never be able to rest for fear of waking up with the knotted cadaver's fists clenched around your throat. You will have to think of a plan or die fighting it. Turn to **240**.

231

As the nearest Spectre charges you take out the vial of holy water which Glaivas gave you and hurl it at the shimmering face of the nearest Spectre Knight. Make an Attack Roll. The Spectre makes no move to protect itself and its Defence is 5. If you hit, turn to **246**. If not, you will have to attack using your martial art skills (turn to **224**).

232

There is no flicker of emotion on Gwyneth's face as she asks you what the fate of the Temple to Dama would be under your Overlordship. You can't tell how interested she is but she may be considering throwing her forces behind you. If you have a pouch of rubies, a potion of healing or a magical rune-carved dagger you can offer them or it to her and say that this is but a small token by comparison with the rewards which will be hers (turn to **220**). Alternatively, you could simply state that you will restore those customs and laws with which your father governed (turn to **208**).

233

You leap into the air and flip backwards into a handstand and then backwards onto your feet again as a viciously spiked club catapults up from its hiding place beneath some rotting leaves to quiver ominously where your chest had been but a moment ago. You take a few moments to regain your composure – you are shaken by your close call. Soon you are on your way and you come to the edge of the wood. Ahead of you, gently rolling ground carpeted in long grass leads to a disorganised pile of chalky rocks and boulders lining the rim of Hunter's Quarry.

Will you head out to examine the quarry – perhaps you can hide there (turn to **204**), or stay where you are and await events (turn to **190**)?

234

You seem to sail through the air, no faster than a cloud crossing the wide firmament, and as your heel moves towards the Fiend's grotesque face its horn-tipped arms close on you in a flash, like pincers, piercing your sides, and you are held above the ground. Lose 9 Endurance. If you are still alive, you hear Glaivas shouting 'Sing, sing a song of gladness against the magic.' If you start to sing, turn to **418**. If not the Fiend casts you to the ground at its cloven hooves. You roll slowly to your feet. You try to flee (turn to **201**).

235

You run as fast as you can and leap towards the plinth. You find yourself in the midst of the flames as they lick and crackle about you, then throw back your head and scream in pain as a thousand needles are driven into every nerve of your body and your mind is seared by an awful heat. You are in so much pain that you can barely move. Desperately you try to force yourself on. If you have any Inner Force left, turn to **247**. If you do not, turn to **265**.

236

You unwind your hood and take a sleeveless white homespun jacket from your bag of ninja tools. To complete your preparations for entering the city, you take off your shoes – the rightful Overlord of Irsmuncast will pass through its gates humbly, barefoot.

The city is set amongst rich farmlands and meadows in

which grow the various plants giving rise to colourful dyes. Irsmuncast is famed throughout the Manmarch for its weaving and dyeing, for carpets, pavilions and tapestry making. It is a fair-seeming city, its walls made of a dull red stone with towers at fifty-foot intervals along the battlements.

As you walk through the fields you can see that its citizens are of many types, some flaxen-haired, others with flashing black eyes and raven hair. You are surprised to see that many of the peasants have a coarse-limbed orcish look about them, and some have the noseless faces of Halvorcs. The Great South Gate is a triumphal arch, topped by two squat towers with a raised portcullis at front and back. The inscription on the arch reads 'In memory of the great victories won by the people of Irsmuncast against the Dark Forces from the Edge'. The gate guard are alert and number ten noseless men, probably Halvorcs, under the command of a priest bearing the whirlpool symbol of Nemesis on his black robes. It seems a strong guard for a city that is not at war. You wait for the influx of peasants at dusk and slip into the city unnoticed at the changing of the guard. Turn to **244**.

237

'What are you?' you demand.

'I am Doré le Jeune, of the order of the Paladin Knights of Dragonhold,' comes the reply.

His name is not a Manmarcher name. Turn to **202**.

238

Your Training of the Heart tells you that the tramp is lying. In fact you see now that the limp is put on and he is not a tramp at all. He darts nervous looks out of the side of his eyes every now and then, but his behaviour is not that of one who feels outcast from society, rather it shows that he fears being found out for what he is. Your Shin-Ren tells you that this is an opportunity to find out more which should not be missed. As you pass a dark doorway you stun him with a deft chop to the back of the neck and drag him into the shadows. As he comes round you slip your garrotte around his neck and tighten it. You can tell he is lying when he says he is a robber and at last he tells you that he is a member of the tyrant's secret informers, responsible for ferreting out all those opposed to the rule of the Usurper. He shows you the yellow mark near his elbow which is carried by all of the tyrant's informers and warns you that they are always to be found in at least two of the larger inns: the Cleansing Flame, frequented solely by followers of Nemesis, and the Hostel from the Edge, where most strangers to the city finish up. When he has told you how to get to the Temple you tighten the wire. He knows too much. His body will not be found till dawn and you hurry back to the Green then turn east. You have struck the first blow against the Usurper. Turn to **269**.

239

A viciously spiked club catapults up from the ground, sending rotten leaves everywhere. You try to twist aside but it catches your shoulder. The impact sends you tumbling to the ground and your shoulder has been gashed open. Lose 4 Endurance. You pick yourself up off the ground and pause for a moment – you have been badly shaken by the unpleasant surprise. Soon you have regained your composure and you continue on until you come to the edge of the wood. Ahead of you, gently rolling ground carpeted in long grass leads to a disorganised pile of chalky rocks and boulders lining the rim of Hunter's Quarry. Will you head out to examine the Quarry – perhaps you can hide there (turn to **204**), or stay where you are and await events (turn to **190**)?

240

You run on, covering mile after mile, and the morning sun banishes the mists. Looking back, you can see the Golem pounding along inexorably a quarter of a mile behind you. It is covering the ground in great strides at a surprising rate. You break into a copse to see if, when it completely loses sight of you, it will give up, but to no avail. The monstrosity pounds on and on towards you. You break cover again and increase your pace, but it seems the Golem will never tire and you begin to sweat. After another hour you are some way ahead and you consider what to do. If you would like to fight it again – perhaps you will be lucky this time and stop it forever – turn to **259**. If you would like to try and enlist some divine aid by praying, turn to **348**. If you would like to plunge into a river to see if it would follow and drown, turn to **270**. If you would like to head for the Mountains of Horn to see if it will fall to destruction, following you as you climb a peak, turn to **357**.

241

The Orcs soon discover their mistake. Glaivas' sword hisses and wherever it travels orcish blood spurts. You punch and kick, felling two immediately, but another of them is stabbing at you with his sword. Your Defence is 6 and if you are hit the Orc inflicts 1 Die damage. If you are still alive, the Orcs turn tail but the Halvorcs are almost upon you and you turn and run. Make a Fate Roll. If Fate smiles on you, turn to **81**. If Fate turns her back on you, turn to **32**.

242

'Golspiel asked me to do a small favour for him,' and he laughs, a chilling sound, filled with evil. Suddenly he snarls. The lips draw back over his teeth and there is a wet tearing sound as, horribly, his jaw elongates, splitting out of his skull. His teeth grow in front of your very eyes, the canines shooting forwards. Fur begins to sprout all over him and his arms and legs crack and shudder, the bones growing, his hands and feet lengthening into taloned paws. His eyes burn with feral ferocity, the pupils changing into cat-like slits, glowing redly. You stand shocked into immobility for a moment as a man becomes a wolf before you. Then the Werewolf throws back his head and howls, a long ululating call, a terrible sound that echoes around the chamber, filling your soul with dread. He drops to all fours and leaps towards you, snarling ferociously. At this you are galvanised into action, virtually a reflex for you now. If you have the skill of Acrobatics and wish to leap above his charge, turn to **341**. If you have a Silver Shuriken or Enchanted Shuriken and wish

to throw it, turn to **200**. Otherwise will you use an Iron Fist punch (turn to **67**), a Forked Lightning kick (turn to **219**) or the Teeth of the Tiger throw (turn to **364**)?

243

Slightly groggy, your movements seem agonizingly slow to you as you move behind the shadow of a tall pine tree. Glaivas' movements, too, seem unnaturally slow as he advances upon the Fiend which alights on the other side of the tree. It turns to Glaivas. Will you flee, reasoning that it has come for you not Glaivas (turn to **201**), or try again to reach the spirit plane, using meditation (turn to **402**)?

244

Once inside the city you decide to seek the safety of the Temple to Kwon, but the street that leads from the gate runs only fifty yards before opening out onto a large green, rutted with the wheels of carts. Oxen teams are being led away from the wagons of a merchant caravan and one corner of the Green is occupied with the gaudily-coloured pavilions of merchants and their agents. One or two smaller tents boast the names of clairvoyants and soothsayers. Two large streets run on from the Green: one, to the north, towards some imposing and grandiose buildings; the other, to the east, towards a park. You dare not ask the way for fear of giving yourself away as a stranger. Will you go north (turn to **254**), go east (turn to **269**) or dally outside one of the soothsayer's booths (turn to **286**)?

245

The needle flies unerringly through the air and slaps into Aiguchi's cheek as he turns to look at you. His eyes widen in horror and he stiffens in pain. Dropping his bow he sinks to his knees, jerking spasmodically. 'You...' he stutters before falling onto his face, dead. You have slain the Weaponmaster without even striking a blow. You walk up to him and search his body. Amongst his weapons you find two bottles. One is filled with a green liquid and is a Potion of Healing. You may drink it at any time and gain up to 10 points of lost

Endurance. The other is filled with a blue liquid and is labelled 'Waters of Protection from Ethereal Flame'. Note these on your Character Sheet. Shouldering Aiguchi's body, you take it with you through the Victor's Gate. Beyond the Gate is a small hut. As you approach it, Maak emerges hurriedly, but pulls up with a look of disappointment on his face as he sees who is dead and who still lives. 'I see you triumphed once again, ninja,' he says angrily. 'By the laws of the Ring you are how free to go. But once you have left this place you will be fair game for your enemies once more. And you have many enemies, ninja.' With that he turns on his heel and walks into the hut. You leave the body of Aiguchi outside the hut and run on, heading for Irsmuncast. Turn to **416**.

246

The vial smashes in the Spectre's face and there is an unearthly scream as the holy water cuts like a powerful acid into the undead monster. It clasps its face in helpless anguish and sets spurs to its warhorse, which promptly bolts, leaving you with only one foe near enough to threaten you, but you have no holy water left. Glaivas is still chanting as the second Spectre charges. It towers above you on its warhorse and you decide to dodge, then launch yourself into a high kick to try and knock it from the saddle. The Spectre's Defence as it tries to claw your leg is 8. If you succeed, turn to **257**. If you fail but are carrying a Saint's Locket, turn to **287**. Otherwise, the cold talons of the Spectre rake your leg and your very life force is drawn from you. Apply −2 to all your Modifiers. If any reach −5, you will be helpless to resist as the life force is drawn out of you and you become a shadow in the service of the Spectre. Until then you can try to kick again (return to the top of this paragraph).

247

The agony is unendurable, but you manage a single step forward. You call upon your innermost reserves of energy and manage to overcome the pain. Deduct 1 from your Inner Force. You dart forward, grab the circlet and hurl yourself back through the flame where you collapse in a heap, panting heavily. But you are unhurt, the pain was only temporary. You stand up and place the circlet on your head, under your hood. It does not feel different in any way, but you know this must be the item you sought (note the Ruby Circlet on your Character Sheet). You leave the circular chamber and find yourself back at the brass-studded oak door. You have little choice but to go through it. Turn to **207**.

248

As you hit the ground your chest begins to burn, as if your lungs were filling with fire. You shut out the pain, but the poison is killing you. Glaivas drags you behind the cover of a myrtle bush and pulls the bolt from your flesh, leaving a gaping wound. Next he takes a piece of waxed paper from a pouch which holds a blue powder, which he then pours into your wound, while speaking a spell of healing. That done, he takes a bone-needle threaded with horsehair and neatly stitches the wound. After a while a cold sweat breaks out on your brow, but the fire in your chest lessens and you can breathe easily once more. The poison was virulent, however, and even with Glaivas' healing you have lost 7 Endurance. Glaivas scouts the hillside for the assassin who all but killed you, but he is long fled. As soon as you are ready to travel on, Glaivas suggests once more that you turn north towards the Forest of Arkadan and says that if you wish to travel through the Valley of the Lich-Kings along the highway you can do so without his help. Will you turn north with Glaivas (turn to **111**) or journey on along the road alone (turn to **136**)?

249

You buy a tankard of ale with a silver coin which you picked up in the park, and sit down next to the young men. Although drunk they are not slow, but you gather they are not altogether happy with their lot, nor are they alone – feelings are running high against the Usurper because he favours a few at the expense of others and seeks to turn friends against each other. They are soon talking to you and one points out the tramp by the door, saying, 'There are several like him. They are the Usurper's secret informers. If he comes this way, talk about the weather.' You are still unsure what their reaction to the possibility of revolution might be so you rack your brains for a way of finding out who might make good allies. Will you say that you have come to Irsmuncast to marry and ask if it is easy to get permission from the Lord High Steward (turn to **263**) or ask how it is the merchant's emporia still look prosperous under the tyrant's rule (turn to **275**)?

250

You arrive at the Victor's Gate without incident. The Gate is right at the wood's end and beyond its flower-adorned stone lies a small wooden hut, presumably where the keepers of the Ring await the winner. You scan the ground carefully; your training in ninjutsu included woodcraft and survival skills and you are happy to find recent tracks leading north-west from the Victor's Gate. It must be Aiguchi. Will you follow the tracks through the Duelwood (turn to **280**) or use this opportunity to make good your escape, by slipping over the Fatestones past the hut and away (turn to **164**)?

251

Astaroth catches you in his claws and hurls you against the statue of the goddess Dama. You land with a sickening thud as your head hits the statue's and lose 3 Endurance. If you are still alive, you may drink a Potion of Healing or use a Bag of Herbs if you have one. At this time, either will restore your Endurance to 20. Astaroth steps back onto the throne and roars 'Scourge, my servant, come to me!' The name Scourge seems to echo dully, as if the Duke of Hell had shouted into a bottomless well. Suddenly a new monster faces you. Astaroth has summoned one of his servants, a Greater Devil, from the Inferno. Scourge has the body of a giant Centaur, but his tail is a mass of writhing serpents and his head is a lion's skull. His steaming flanks drip black blood. Scourge roars and gallops to the attack and you are hard put to defend yourself, while Astaroth lolls at ease on the throne. You decide to use kicks against Scourge as he is too tall for

punches to really affect him. You can only use Kwon's Flail if you have the knowledge of it.

SCOURGE THE CENTAUR DEVIL
Defence against Leaping Tiger kick: 7
Defence against Kwon's Flail: 5
Damage 2 Dice + 2
Endurance: 22

Your blows affect Scourge as if he were a normal beast, while he is not in hell, but Inner Force does not affect him. The Saint's Locket and the Ruby Circlet will protect you against Scourge as they did against Astaroth, as the Centaur Devil rears and smashes down his iron hooves to stave in your skull. Your Defence as you try to leap aside is 7, or 8 if you have the skill of Acrobatics. If you have survived two of his attacks, turn to **229**. If not, and you are still alive, fight Scourge again.

252

You succeed only in putting your arms before your face, and the blackhawk's talons rip into them instead. Your arm muscles will heal badly and you must apply −1 to your Punch Modifier. You strike out, but the great bird is soaring skyward once more and the Orcs are upon you.

Turn to **241**.

253

Racing to the attack, you pivot and deliver a finely-judged strike against the nerve point in the Duke of Hell's side, but the blow does not affect him. He is immune to Yubi-Jutsu in his true form. You spring back, but a scything claw rakes your shoulder. Lose 2 Endurance.

If you have the skill of Poison Needles, you may wish to use one – turn to **336**. Otherwise you must rely on your more straightforward martial arts skills – turn to **320**, as the devil roars and attacks.

The city is quite busy and large torches burn at the corners of the streets, but it appears that each house is obliged to hang a lantern outside its door to light the way. The people hurry home, heads bowed. There is a mood of spineless dejection everywhere. A group of figures wearing chainmail marches towards you and you see to your surprise that they are Orcs. Their shields are emblazoned with red deer with barbed tails and spiralling horns. You move aside and they march on, ignoring you. The street leads past shops and stalls which have been shut up for the night. At its end is a small palace set in a high-walled garden with regimented flower beds. The pointed towers at either end fly two flags: one is the same device that emblazoned the orcish shields, the other the black whirlpool of Nemesis. You are looking at the Usurper's Palace, soon you hope to be your own. It is very heavily guarded by men, Orcs and wardogs. It will not be easy to gain entry. If you have the skill of Climbing and wish to do so as the night deepens, turn to **96**. If you decide to retrace your steps, turn to **109**.

You put a small poison-tipped needle onto your rolled tongue, then spit it at the rippling silvered chest of the Fiend as it is about to crush you with its horny-armed embrace. The needle flies true but the monster seems not even to realise what has happened. You dive aside but too slowly, and one of its arms catches you a scything blow and you lose 5 Endurance. If you still live, turn to **396**.

Your fingers are probing the hippogriff-decorated depression when there is a click and grinding noise. The door-like slab begins to sink into the floor. Suddenly there is another sound and the floor beneath your feet abruptly gives way and you fall down into a pit some fifteen feet deep. You land painfully and lose 2 Endurance. If you are still alive, you have dropped your torch and it is pitch black. Feeling around you find yourself in a pit about six feet in diameter. Its walls are of soft earth. Looking up you can see a circle of bright light. Whatever was behind the secret entrance is giving off a lot of light. If you have the skill of Climbing, turn to **297**. If you do not, turn to **315**.

257

Even though you can see right through the body of the Spectre it is substantial enough. There is a great thump as it hits the ground and the warhorse bolts, but the Spectre seems unhurt, getting to its feet and reaching for you with its taloned hands. Will you try to throw it, then follow up with a Winged Horse kick (turn to **224**), use an Iron Fist punch (turn to **307**) or a Leaping Tiger kick (turn to **313**)?

258

As Aiguchi turns, the needle falls at his feet, spent before it has reached him. He starts at the sight of you and then says, 'Using your filthy tricks to get behind me, eh! I'll make you pay for that.' Reaching for his curve-bladed spear or naginata, he leaps towards you, whirling it about his head in an amazing display of martial skill. You can see he is fast, very fast, as you back away from him. He begins to edge towards you, crab-like, the tip of his spear always pointed, unerringly, at your throat. You circle each other. Suddenly he hops and thrusts the spear at your belly with great speed, but you sweep it aside with your arm. For a brief moment you are inside the reach of the naginata. If you have the skill of Yubi-Jutsu, you realise he is too quick for you to use a precision nerve-strike, and you will have to slow him down first. Will you try the Leaping Tiger kick (turn to **56**), the Teeth of the Tiger throw (turn to **22**), a Tiger's Paw chop (turn to **38**) or wait for a suitable moment and, using Inner Force, attempt to snap Aiguchi's naginata (turn to **10**)?

259

You stand your ground once more and the monster lumbers toward you, showing no signs of fatigue. The sickly-sweet smell almost makes you gag at the thought of doing battle with it again. You are still tired from battle and flight. Will you use the Leaping Tiger kick (turn to **165**), the Tiger's Paw chop (turn to **179**) or the Winged Horse (turn to **191**)?

260

You dodge nimbly to Astaroth's side but as you do so a cloud of steam hisses from his nostrils, almost boiling you alive. You lose 4 Endurance before you can strike. If you still live, you may attack.

ASTAROTH THE SEVENTH DUKE OF HELL
Defence against Tiger's Paw chop: 8
Endurance: 33
Damage: 3 Dice

If you have hit Astaroth for the first time, turn to **412**. Otherwise you are forced back under a fusillade of death-dealing blows. Your Defence against Astaroth's champing jaws is 6. If you are wearing a Saint's Locket, it protects you and you lose 3 less Endurance than the dice show if Astaroth hits you. If you are wearing a Ruby Circlet, this also protects you and you lose 4 less Endurance than the dice show. If you survive and have now tried to kick and/or punch twice, turn to **251**. Otherwise, you may chop again (return to the top of this paragraph) or try a kick (turn to **267**).

261

The bolt has gashed your chest badly and the poison on its tip causes an unwelcome warmness close to your heart, but your years of training with poisons has meant that your body has developed immunity to the venom and you are untroubled by it. Glaivas pulls the bolt from your flesh, leaving a gaping wound. The signs of poison on the bolt are plain to him and he takes a piece of waxed paper from a pouch, but you tell him he need not concern himself with the poison. 'So the tales they tell of the ninja are true,' he says, smiling. You reply that there are many secrets unknown about the ninja as well. Glaivas seems about to say something but takes a bone-needle threaded with horsehair from his belt instead and, after saying a spell of healing, stitches up your wound. His skill is such that you have lost only 1 point of Endurance. There is no sign of your assailant; Glaivas suggests once more that you turn north towards the Forest of Arkadan and says that if you wish to travel through the Valley of the Lich-Kings along the highway you can do so without his help. Will you turn north with Glaivas (turn to **111**) or journey on along the road alone (turn to **136**)?

262

You leap high and kick powerfully, but you are not quick enough to beat the blade. The silvery sword arcs around and catches your leg, shearing through flesh to bone. If you have the Acrobatics skill, turn to **279**. If not, you are knocked aside, stunned, and the horse rears above you before bringing its hooves down upon your head splitting your skull. If you had not been still drowsy after your long sleep you would not have been caught by the magical sword, but you have met your match at the edge of the Rift.

263

'That depends,' says one of the young men, on whether you worship at the Temple to Nemesis.' 'Or the Temple to Time,' puts in another. 'Oh yes, or Time,' agrees the first. 'Why Time?' you ask. 'Everyone knows the priests of Time don't care an hour-candle as to who rules the city, as long as they are left alone to pursue their strange devotions. They are powerful to be sure, but did they do anything when the Loremaster was murdered by that monk? No!' As the conversation goes on you see how the Temple to Time enjoys great privileges in return for not opposing the Usurper. One of the men rolls dead-drunk under the bench and they haul him to his feet and leave – you decide to do the same as the tramp sidles towards the emptying bench. Turn to **6**.

264

As you run Glaivas says that there are guard huts all around the hedge, which is twenty miles round. Wherever you try to scale it you will have to fight so he suggests you run east, the way you wish to go, avoiding as much trouble as you can.

Twice you turn south to avoid new parties of guards until it feels as though a multitude of Orcs and Halvorcs are closing in from all sides, and still the blackhawk circles above you. At last you see the other side of the Palisade of Thorns and sprint through the rippling corn, before any guards stationed there can group together to repulse or capture you. As the hedge looms near you are startled as a row of ten Halvorcs rise suddenly from crouching positions in the corn. You are running towards their spear points. If you have the skill of Arrow Cutting, turn to **196**. If not, one of them hurls his spear, which catches you in the thigh. You pluck it out but the wound bleeds. Lose 5 Endurance. If you are still alive, turn to **187**.

265

You take a single step forward but the agony is unendurable. Even your superlative training is not enough to help you resist the pain. Against your wishes your body steps back out of the flames, where you collapse in a heap, panting heavily. But you are unhurt, the pain was only temporary. Knowing it will be impossible for you to pass through the flames, you turn away from the circlet dejectedly. You will have to prevail against the Usurper without any such help. You come to the brass-studded oak door. You have little choice but to pass through. Turn to **207**.

266

You strike northwards, following the path. You move unseen and unheard until you arrive at the edge of the Duelwood. Ahead of you, gently rolling ground carpeted in long grass leads to a disorganised pile of chalky rocks and boulders lining the rim of Hunter's Quarry. Will you head out to examine the Quarry – perhaps you can hide there (turn to **204**), or stay where you are and await events (turn to **190**)?

267

Astaroth stalks towards you and as you move in to strike, a torrent of hail pours from his mouth in a wide jet. The battering chill saps your energy. Lose 4 Endurance. If you are still alive, you can attack. If you have played Book 1: *AVENGER!* and learnt Kwon's Flail, you may add a further 2 points to the damage inflicted if you succeed.

ASTAROTH THE SEVENTH DUKE OF HELL
Defence against Winged Horse kick: 9
Defence against Kwon's Flail: 8
Endurance: 33
Damage: 3 Dice

If you have hit Astaroth for the first time, turn to **412**. Otherwise you are forced back under a fusillade of death-dealing blows. Your Defence against Astaroth's mighty claws is 5. If you are wearing a Saint's Locket, it protects you and you lose 3 less Endurance than the dice show if Astaroth hits you. If you are wearing a Ruby Circlet, this also protects you and you lose 4 less Endurance than the dice show.

If you survive and have now tried to kick and/or punch twice, turn to **251**. Otherwise, you can kick again (return to the top of this paragraph) or try the Tiger's Paw chop (turn to **260**).

268

You do not have long to wait. Four figures on horseback approach at a slow walk. Their countenances are cruel and they seem to look upon you with contempt. You can see right through them, and their clothes, once gaudy martial finery, are now no more than a ghostly shimmering, but the might of their evil intelligence is almost palpable as they advance to take you. Grizell screams and then faints, overcome with terror. Her body rolls down the slope towards them, while Glaivas unravels a scroll of parchment and begins to chant. One of them dismounts beside Grizell, while the other charges you. The Spectre stoops over the slave girl and draws the life out of her body with a touch.

If you wish to attack using your martial arts straight away, turn to **224**. If you wish to try some other form of attack, turn to **231**.

The main street leading east is called the Edgeway. It leads past the houses of well-to-do people towards the park which is surrounded by railings and with two huge iron gates. A grisly sight meets your eye. In the flickering torches you see the bodies of a woman and a man who have been whipped and then broken on the wheel. Their hands and feet have been stretched wide and roped to the edges of the huge wheel which might once have carried a catapult. She was evidently a shieldmaiden, he unmistakably a monk of Kwon. Placards are nailed to the tree trunks to which the wheels are fixed, bearing the word, 'Traitors'. It seems they have died for opposing the Usurper. You walk past the bloodied bodies into the park. A glow of many torches lights up a cloistered monastery adjoining a great church to Kwon the Redeemer. You walk to the monastery gate where a monk greets you and you tell him who you are. A glimpse at your birthmark is enough to convince him that you are Avenger and he leads you to meet the High Grandmaster, who is at prayer in a small private chapel. Turn to **181**.

You flee to the east many more miles until at last you come to the banks of the river Fortune winding between the spurs of the hills. It is wide, deep and fast-flowing but it will pose no danger to you, for you swim like a fish. You catch your breath as the monster approaches, then dive into the dark green depths of the river. At the bottom you wait; if you have the skill of Feigning Death, you prepare by slowing your heart until your body needs almost no oxygen. Then a great death-white fleshy hand reaches out for you. You surge backwards as the Golem almost grabs you and begin to swim downstream under water. The monster is carrying a large stone as ballast and it strides powerfully through the watery gloom. It does not need air to breathe; you will have to devise a new plan. You shoot upwards to the surface and drag yourself onto the bank just inches before the grasping hands, then begin to run once more. Your breathing is painful and you lose 3 Endurance unless you have the skill of Feigning

Death. If you are still alive, will you fight the monster again (turn to **259**)? If you would rather pray, turn to **348**. If you wish to head for the Mountains of Horn in the hope that it will fall to its destruction while climbing a peak after you, turn to **357**.

271

Kiyamo and Onikaba are pleased to see you and they thank you again for aiding them, and for ridding the Island of Plenty of one of the ninja of the Way of the Scorpion. Kiyamo asks you how he can be of service to you, saying he is forever in your debt, for you saved the Island of Plenty by slaying the demon, Jikkyu. You tell him of your quest to regain the throne of Irsmuncast.

'Your destiny is indeed great, Avenger, and I shall do all in my power to aid you,' he replies. 'I will provide you with a ship to take you to the Manmarch, but as you must overthrow the Usurper of Irsmuncast, it seems to me you will also need some warriors to aid you. I shall give you one hundred samurai warriors, led by Onikaba. It will take time to organise the expedition but I will send them after you as soon as I am able. With luck they will arrive at Irsmuncast in time to be of use.'

Onikaba smiles and says, 'I would be honoured to serve under you, Avenger.'

Kiyamo unfolds a map of the Manmarch on the table and says, 'I know little of the Manmarch, Avenger. Will you have Onikaba and the warrior army land near Doomover and march to Irsmuncast, obviously the quickest route – but is it the safest? Or will you have him land at Tor and march up the Valley of the Lich-Kings? The decision is yours, after all, he is now yours to command,' and he smiles at you. Make your decision and note on your Character Sheet which route you wish the samurai to take to Irsmuncast. Kiyamo orders that a ship be prepared for you and takes his leave, saying, 'May Fate smile on you, Avenger,' and Onikaba and an escort of ten samurai lead you to the port of Lemné.

'I shall be with you again soon, Lord,' Onikaba says and bows to you. You wish him well and thank him before boarding the sloop that awaits you, the *Sea Dragon*.

The captain asks you where you wish to be taken. Will you travel towards Doomover and thence to Irsmuncast, the more direct route (turn to **330**) or to Tor, where Glaivas the Ranger-Lord lives and thence to Irsmuncast (turn to **21**)?

272

You mis-time your swipe and the quarrel flies under your sleeve-guard and into your chest, knocking you to the ground. If you have Immunity to Poisons, turn to **261**. If not, turn to **248**.

273

Leaving the clearing and the Barrow Mound, you pad silently up the path, hugging its edges, making sure you cannot be seen easily. Soon you come to the crossroads in the midst of the murky Duelwood. You pause, listening and searching for tracks, but you can detect no sign of Aiguchi. Will you head east towards the Victor's Gate (turn to **250**) or north (turn to **266**)?

274

The throwing star blurs through the air, and the shuriken embeds itself in the golden breast plate with a clank. The figure seems unmoved but there is the faintest trickle of blood from the smiling face mask and then a coughing sound. It clamps a metalled fist to its chest, rips out the star and hurls it into the Rift, where it falls from sight. Next it seems to speak a garbled message, then it draws the bastard sword, which glows with a silver radiance. You decide to dodge aside, and try to knock it from the saddle with a Leaping Tiger kick (turn to **262**).

275

'If anyone can survive a tyrant, it's a merchant,' says one of the young men. 'Those silver-tongued spawn of the Rift always have a trick up their sleeves. Me, I don't trust them as far as I can spit.' You are unable to find out how the merchants have managed this but it seems that Golspiel, their spokesman, has done particularly well. One of the young men suggests he is in favour because he knows how to procure the things the Usurper most desires, but he falls dead-drunk under the table before he can go on. The others haul him to his feet and leave. You decide to do the same as the tramp sidles towards the emptying bench. Turn to **6**.

276

As the Fiend spreads its horned arms in a ghastly embrace, you snatch a glance at the Guardian Angel. Its face is set and determined but it is a lawful being and it will obey only the command of the god Avatar and his Consort Illustra to guard the gateway of the Seven Heavens against all comers. You see the regret in its face as it takes the hard decision to leave you in the lap of Fate. You strike out but cannot prevent the powerful horns closing around you, then all goes dark. The terrible ringing of the great bell of Dis, the Iron-city of the Underworld, reverberates around your skull. All around you is cold iron. You have been carried away to hell where you will suffer eternal torment.

277

Using your power of mind over matter, you force yourself to ignore the threat that seems about to confront you and relax utterly. The root has freed your mind from the ties of belief which bind it to your body and your spirit flies free. You feel yourself floating gently upwards and below you can see Glaivas and the top of your own head, but Glaivas cannot see you. Your spirit is home away suddenly by a gust of ethereal wind. In sudden panic you realise that you can hardly help yourself here on the spirit plane but you dimly sense pathways stretching through the ether. A dark shape looms behind you. The beast, whatever it is, has managed to follow you onto the spirit plane. The wind whirls you towards a parting of ways and something tells you that the right-hand path leads towards the gates of heaven, whilst the left leads towards the Elysian Fields. You struggle to take one of the paths. Will you take the right path (turn to **295**) or the left (turn to **302**)?

You journey northwards for two days, skirting to the east of a range of wooded hills, and then the ground begins to dip. In the distance ahead are tall black cliffs and the vegetation gives way to rocky earth which is blackened and cracked, then an immense chasm opens up before you. You have gone too far east and stumbled across the Bowels of Orb, the great Rift, spawn of all evil, that opens on the middle of the Manmarch. You are in the most dangerous region on all of Orb. As you walk away from the edge of the precipice a great geyser of gas and sand erupts and noxious vapours overcome you, forcing you into a deep sleep.

You lie dead to the world in this most dangerous region for a day and a night. When you reawaken you are shocked to realise how long you have slept in the steaming desolation at the yawning edge of the chasm. Yet you are well: you may restore up to 4 points of lost Endurance for your rest. You stretch then look around. To the west, green and forested hills; to the north, the fissured bleakness of baked mud and black rock that lines the Bowels of Orb. Still feeling drowsy, you set off north-west anxious to leave the chasm behind. There is no telling what evil may issue forth to assail you at any time. Turn to **339**.

You are knocked aside but you manage to land on your hands and flip to your feet. You have lost 2 Endurance from the sword cut. You break for cover towards dense forest. The figure gallops after you, but the trees are so close together that the horse is slowed down and you make good your escape. Your pulse quickens as you come upon a cave amongst the trees. There are unusual statues of small woodland creatures in lifelike attitudes littered around and the smell of quicklime gives you the clue that a basilisk lurks within.

You hurry on, not wishing to be caught in the basilisk's stare and become a statue yourself. At the forest's edge you strike north. Turn to **199**.

The tracks go through the dark murk of the Duelwood. After a while they lead you to the edge of the trees. Ahead of you, gently rolling ground, carpeted in long grass, leads to a disorganised pile of chalky rocks and boulders lining the rim of Hunter's Quarry. You can see that the tracks lead in the general direction of the quarry. Will you stay where you are and await events (turn to **190**) or move out towards the quarry (turn to **204**)?

The speeding bolt is only a few feet from your chest when you catch sight of it, but you whip your forearm across its path with split-second timing. The metal bolt clangs on your iron sleeve-guard, then spins harmlessly away into a myrtle bush.

Glaivas is on his feet and sprinting around behind the hill immediately. You retrieve the bolt and run up the other side of the hill, but meet Glaivas at the summit without having glimpsed your unknown enemy. The crossbow bolt is grooved and there is poison on it – the assassins are at work again. Glaivas suggests once more that you turn north towards the Forest of Arkadan and says that if you wish to travel through the Valley of the Lich-Kings along the highway you can do so without his help. Will you turn north with Glaivas (turn to **111**) or journey on along the road alone (turn to **136**)?

You fall back towards the pine trees until your foot is jerked out from under you and you are hauled upside down into the air. You have stepped in a trapper's snare which was attached by a length of rope to a bent bough of a pine. Now the rope dangles you upside down before Honoric. There is a look of fury in his eyes, and Sorcerak smokes inches from your unprotected neck. You prepare to try to block its blow but Honoric is merely staring hard into your eyes. Your gaze is unflinching as you look death in the face but there is not a glimmer of fear in your eye. Honoric speaks, 'I have been cheated by a mere trapper's snare.'

Sorcerak whines through the air and you fall, momentarily stunned, to the ground. As you shake your head to clear your senses, you see Honoric mount his warhorse and ride off. He has spared your life. Instead of killing you, he cut the rope that held you dangling from the tree. You free yourself from the snare and continue on your way, shaking your head in wonder. Turn to **13**.

283

You rush the Fiend together as it becomes flesh and blood before you and there is a banshee wail, 'Aiee, it pains me so to journey to this plane of life.' It is still adjusting to its surroundings when Glaivas' sword buries itself into one of its wings and you drive a Leaping Tiger kick at its face. There is a faint noise like the Death-Knell of the great bell in the Iron-city of Dis deep in the Underworld. Note that you have heard a Death-Knell. Things seem to speed up all around and, for a moment, your own movements become agonizingly slow, then it passes and you duck beneath a scything swing of the Fiend's horn-tipped arm. To your dismay neither your kick nor the Ranger's sword seem even to have marked the Fiend's skin. Glaivas calls, 'There is nothing we can do to harm it. It cannot stay too long on this plane, follow me,' and with that he begins to run. Will you follow (turn to **209**) or stay to fight (turn to **197**)?

284

You do not have long to wait. Four figures on horseback approach at a slow walk. Their countenances are cruel and they seem to look upon you with contempt. You can see right through them, and their clothes, once gaudy martial finery, are now no more than a ghostly shimmering, but the might of their evil intelligence is almost palpable as they advance to take you. Glaivas unravels a scroll of parchment and begins to chant as two of them charge you.

If you wish to attack using your martial arts straight away, turn to **224**. If you wish to try some other form of attack, turn to **231**.

Using thought alone, you wish yourself into the windstream of ether that pours past the gateway. The Guardian Angel recedes quickly into the distance, but the Fiend from the Pit bears down on you, its horny arms spread wide to engulf you in a ghastly embrace. Suddenly a sinuous form takes shape in the ether before you. It is a perfect tiger, but her fur is white and her eyes blue, the Spirit Tiger, servant of Kwon the Redeemer. The Fiend's face creases in feral rage as it realises it has been denied its quarry even at the instant of the kill. The magnificent Spirit Tiger, flawless and powerful, launches herself at the grisly Fiend and a bloody battle begins. The usually calm Spirit Tiger bites and rakes her claws at the Fiend with bestial ferocity although her head is belaboured by crushing blows from the arms of horn. At last the Fiend from the Pit realises that death is about to take it. The horns score deep furrows down the Spirit Tiger's flank but her jaws finally meet in the Fiend's neck. Its grisly form shrivels and is gone. Just its soul like a blackened and shrivelled grub is left to be carried back to the Underworld on the ethereal wind. You are about to offer prayers and thanks to the Spirit Tiger when, far away, the Guardian Angel speaks a single word, 'Llandymion', and you find your mind pouring itself back into your inert body. Glaivas starts with relief as he sees you move again, for your body has been absolutely still. You tell him what has happened and settle down once more to take what rest you can, free of the feeling of malice that had so darkened your thoughts of late. You rise the next day and continue your journey. Turn to **414**.

You step across the rutted Green towards a booth decked out in scarlet and blue which boasts the name, 'Lucretia, enchantress and Seer of the South, Knower of Secrets Unknown'. You duck under an awning, into a gloomy tent lined with worn tapestries depicting an artisan's imagining of the Garden of the Gods. Kwon the Redeemer is given prominent place between Eo and Avatar. The woman hunched over an enormous crystal ball has a face so wrinkled and folded you wonder that she can see out of it, but, then, you reflect, perhaps she has no need of vision as you know it. She does not look up but asks you to sit on a worn velvet-covered stool.

'Time waits for no one, no one should wait for Time,' she says mysteriously, then in an altogether different voice, 'Cross my palm with gold, then.' If you wish to give her money, turn to **362**. Otherwise, turn to **319**.

287

One of the Spectre's taloned claws catches you and you feel your life force ebbing away, but then the cold talon touches the Locket which Grizell gave you. It truly contains a lock of saint's hair and the Spectre recoils as if burnt. You whip out the Locket and the Spectre turns to flee. Glaivas' scroll seems to have banished one of his foes which turns to dust in moments – he has cast a Raise the Dead spell on the long undead warlord, whose body suffered the decay of centuries in seconds. The fourth Spectre turns tail and gallops after his fleeing companions. You have fought against members of the Spectral Company and lived, but Grizell is beyond help. The magic from the Ranger's scroll is spent and you must leave her frail body to rot. Glaivas hopes that you will escape the other members of the Company for you would surely die now if found by them. You skirt the mountains, entering the wilderness at dawn. You have travelled through the Valley of the Lich-Kings, from one end to the other. Turn to **299**.

288

Too late, you realise that you haven't time to reach the state of mind which might allow your spirit to float free from the shackles of your body. You dive aside instead but too slowly, and one of the Fiend's arms catches you a scything blow. Lose 5 Endurance. If you still live, turn to **396**.

289

Aiguchi staggers back from your last blow, sorely wounded, his face a mask of agony. Desperately he backs away and reaches into his jacket and draws out a small bottle full of green liquid. You turn to attack but he gives ground fast, the long spear held in one hand enough to keep you at distance whilst he quaffs the contents of the bottle. It is a magical healing potion for in front of your very eyes his wounds are closing up and his bruises fading. He grins with renewed vigour and hefts his naginata with new strength, laughing. You sigh in dismay as he draws close to you, for you will have to fight him all over again. Suddenly he drives the butt of his spear into the ground and pole vaults at you, feet first. Your Defence is 8 against his drop kick. If you are hit, he takes you in the chest and you are sent sprawling backwards. Lose 2 Endurance. If you are still alive, as he turns to face you, you have an opportunity to attack. You decide against trying to snap the naginata, for you have no wish to see what other tricks he has waiting. Will you use the Winged Horse kick (turn to **145**), the Dragon's Tail throw (turn to **76**) or an Iron Fist punch (turn to **117**)?

Your keen senses, honed to perfection by years of training, enable you to pick out slight discolouration on the far wall. Examining it closely you find a small opening in line with the small depression in the middle of the door-like slab. Carefully, you probe the hippogriff-decorated depression with your fingers. Suddenly there is a click, but, forewarned, you throw yourself to the floor immediately. A crossbow bolt flies from the opposite wall to shatter against the stone slab where your back was an instant ago. Then there is a grinding sound and the door-like slab begins to sink into the ground. Bright light floods out from the room beyond. Walking through the secret entrance, you find yourself in a large circular chamber. Immediately before you on the ground is a stone slab, the resting place of a long-dead Lord of Irsmuncast. In the centre of the room stands a marble plinth surrounded by a ring of flames. Upon the plinth rests a thin gold circlet. It is adorned with a single sparkling ruby that glitters in the light. This must be the item you were told would be of use against the Usurper. You cannot discern what the flames are feeding off – indeed there is something very odd about the fire. It gives off a bright white light and the flames flicker and burn about an inch off the ground. They are a coppery yellow and seem insubstantial in some way. Stepping closer you quickly pass your hand through the flame. An agonizing pain fills your soul for an instant, burning at the core of your being. You realise that these are not physical flames but ethereal flames, and that they would not leave your clothes and skin charred and blackened, but your very soul itself. Do you have a bottle containing 'Waters of Protection from Ethereal Flame'? If you do, turn to **225**. If you do not, turn to **212**.

After many weeks your new training is over and the Grandmaster of the Dawn summons you to the Temple. In the meditation room you let your spirits roam free together and your mind is wafted away by the ethereal wind. The Grandmaster travels with you and, to your surprise, you see that his ethereal form is that of a smiling young woman, crowned with a halo of burning silver. He leads you onward; you grasp the milk-white, smooth-skinned hand and hold on tightly. For all your training, you would drift helplessly without guidance.

The Grandmaster of the Dawn points ahead as you approach a gleaming archway, the Gateway to the Seven Heavens. There are other beings here: cherubs flocking about the pillars of the arch and a Guardian Angel, flawless and white. Then beyond, on the silver pathway which stretches up into the clouds, you see a sinuous shape. 'We are here to speak to her,' says the Grandmaster. 'She will come to you as you have need; we may not enter ourselves.'

The form glides past the Guardian Angel, and as it approaches, you see that it is a perfect tiger, but her fur is white and her eyes are blue. The Spirit Tiger looks at you and passes on a part of her knowledge. It is a warning. The evil gods are angry, and, in your struggle against the Usurper, Kwon may not help you. You must triumph through your own sagacity and strength of hand.

Just as the Spirit Tiger is turning away, she pauses to look into your eyes again and you hear her voice in your mind, 'Although the Great Redeemer will not aid you directly, I am his servant and I will strive to protect you from the malice of the gods of evil for they are summoning fell creatures to thwart you.' With that she is gone and you are swept up in the ethereal wind, returning at last to the Temple where your mind rejoins your body.

Turn to **80**.

292

She is in her middle years, gaunt of face but strong-looking, and there is a scar across the bridge of her nose. Her manner of speaking as she directs you on your way is like that of a drill master. She strides on purposefully into the darkness, her hand on her sword hilt. It seems you must go back to the Green and then turn east towards the park.

It is quite dark by the time you reach the Green once more. Turn to **269**.

293

As you fall back you notice that you have been lucky to miss a snare attached to one of the pine trees and you pull up as you notice another behind you. You put the first trap between you and Honoric, hoping that he will blunder into it. Your resourcefulness is rewarded as the snare tightens around his ankle and a bent pine bough whips upright, pulling him off his feet. He hangs upside down before your face, the trapper's snare dangling him from the tree. But he hasn't lost his presence of mind. 'Bear me aloft, Sorcerak,' he shouts, and his body floats out of your reach. He hangs grimly onto the hilt of his sword which pulls him into the topmost leaves of the tree. A leather pouch falls from his belt, which you scoop up quickly as you hear the sound of many hooves cresting a hill nearby. It is a strong party of Legion of the Sword of Doom. You decide to make good an escape while you can as Honoric blusters furiously, 'You mock me Fate, it was not destined to end like this!' but his cries are soon far behind you and his men try to calm him down. You will have to run fast and far to avoid them. Turn to **3**.

294

You walk around the Barrow Mound, senses alert for any oddities. Do you have the skill of Picking Locks, Detecting and Disarming Traps? If so, turn to **328**. If not, turn to **345**.

295

Somehow your mind gropes its way to the right-hand path and then the ethereal wind bowls you onwards. Behind you is a dark shadow which looms ever larger, the spirit of the Fiend from the Pit. It travels the byways of the ether as easily as you would walk down a flagged road. Ahead of you is a gleaming archway beyond which a silver pathway stretches up into white clouds. Cherubs who once flocked around its pillars are racing away up the silver path, but the Guardian Angel of the Gateway to the Seven Heavens stands resolute. He is clad in flawless white armour from head to foot, and his face is like that of a saintly Paladin. 'You may not pass.'

His voice sounds a sorrowful but dire warning. The Fiend from the Pit is taking shape behind you once more and the Guardian Angel looks grimly determined, feet braced wide on the steps to the Gateway. The feet of your silvery ethereal form are on the bottom step. Will you tell the Guardian Angel that you seek the Spirit Tiger (turn to **306**), try to slip past the Guardian Angel using whatever skills you have, perhaps Acrobatics, (turn to **318**) or call the Spirit Tiger as loudly as you can (turn to **331**)?

296

You tell the High Grandmaster that you intend to approach the Swordswomen of Dama, and he tells you a little about them. Their belief is in law and order and they believe that only through discipline and the taming of the havoc-wreaking elements will life on Orb realise its full potential. They do not see good as being in itself preferable to evil, though they are by no means evil. He sends a messenger to tell the Force-Lady Gwyneth that you are on your way to see her.

Soon you are in Cross Street, slipping into the large church of grey stone, which looks like a fort, and are led by two swordswomen up the many stairs to the top tier of the Keep. One of the women knocks on a door and a strong voice says, 'Enter'. You are ushered in and come face to face with Force-Lady Gwyneth. She has a determined look, hands calloused from swordplay and short spiky iron-grey hair. She looks at ease in well-worn armour.

You tell her who you are and show her your father's hippogriff seal and, when she asks, your birthmark. She asks you about your life and you tell her, dwelling on your enmity with Honoric and the Legion of the Sword of Doom. When you tell her that you are going to kill the Usurper and lead a revolution she merely nods. Will you say that you value the trusty sword-arms of her soldiers and ask her to fight against a rule whose end result will be chaos (turn to **232**) or say that with her soldiers, victory is assured and that you will make her general in chief of the forces of Irsmuncast when you are Overlord (turn to **214**)?

You hurl your grappling hook out of the pit until it has locked securely into the floor of the room above. A moment later you are standing at the top of the pit, looking into the room beyond the now-opened stone door. Bright light floods out from it and you step through it. You find yourself in a large circular chamber. Immediately before you on the ground is a stone slab, the resting place of a long-dead Lord of Irsmuncast. In the centre of the room stands a marble plinth surrounded by a ring of flames. Upon the plinth rests a thin gold circlet. It is adorned with a single sparkling ruby that glitters in the light. This must be the item you were told would be of use against the Usurper. You cannot discern what the flames are feeding off – indeed there is something very odd about the fire. It gives off a bright white light and the flames flicker and burn about an inch off the ground. The flames are a coppery yellow and seem insubstantial in some way. Stepping closer you quickly pass your hand through the flame. An agonizing pain fills your soul for an instant, burning at the core of your being. You realise that these are not physical flames but ethereal flames and that they would not leave your clothes and skin charred and blackened, but your very soul itself. Do you have a bottle containing 'Waters of Protection from Ethereal Flame'? If you do, turn to **225**. If you do not, turn to **212**.

You race up the steps to the throne and then leap and drive a powerful kick towards the Usurper's face. But the quickness of his reactions takes you by surprise. He sweeps his arm across into your leg and the power of the blow is far beyond that of any man. You hurtle thirty feet through the air, towards the wall of the Throne Room. If you are skilled in Acrobatics, you hit the wall feet first and then cartwheel to your feet, losing only 2 Endurance. If not, you crash against the wall and then fall to the floor, losing 4 Endurance. If you are still alive, as you look again at the Usurper a hideous transformation takes place. The Usurper's flesh turns red and bloated. Then spikes start to grow out of his back with a noise of tearing flesh. Before your very eyes the Usurper is turning into a Duke of Hell. As you stare, transfixed, he has grown huge bat-like wings, terrible claws and fangs. His face transformed is a mask of hellish evil, far beyond the petty malevolence of mortals. If you have the skill of Poison Needles and wish to use one, turn to **336**. If you decide to attack again using your martial arts, but with more care, turn to **320**.

299

You run on through the day and, looking back, you see several grey figures on magnificent black horses following your trail. There are seven of them and as they begin to catch you up you can see it is the other six of the Spectral Company, Ganarre at their head. You sprint towards a line of white boundary stones topped with black pitch and down a slope beyond. Looking back you see that the Spectres have reined in at the boundary and now stare balefully as you flee. They do not pass the line of stones but they watch until you are beyond the horizon. You have escaped them. Glaivas guides you past the city of Greydawn, counselling you not to risk your life by entering the city, and at last you turn north past the Mountains of Horn. Glaivas has decided to return to Tor across the Manmarch. At the parting of ways, Glaivas gives you a beautiful Silver Shuriken and he kisses your forehead, wishing you luck and the wisdom of long years. Then he is gone leaving no trail, as you call your thanks. Note the Silver Shuriken on your Character Sheet. You may use it as a normal shuriken if you have need. Turn to **278**.

300

You climb up the grassy knoll until you are beside the Pillar of Death. It towers about fifteen feet above you. Looking around you see that you are on about the same level as the trees of the Duelwood. The runes on the pillar are in some archaic language indecipherable to you, but they seem to radiate menace. If you have the skill of Climbing you may try to scale the menhir (turn to **312**). If not or if you do not wish to, will you climb down the Mound and head for Victor's

Gate (turn to **250**), follow the path north to the crossroads (turn to **273**) or climb down the slopes and examine the Mound (turn to **294**)?

301

You break towards a dense patch of forest and the figure reins in, motionless once more, until you disappear from sight. You press on through thick forest and your pulse quickens as you come upon a cave amongst the trees. There are unusual statues of small woodland creatures in lifelike attitudes littered around. The smell of quicklime gives you a clue that a basilisk lurks within. You hurry on, not wishing to be caught in the basilisk's stare and become a statue yourself. At the forest's edge you strike north. Turn to **199**.

302

Somehow your mind gropes its way to the left-hand path and then the ethereal wind blows you onward. Before you lie the Elysian Fields, paradise. But it is ringed by a tall unbroken wall of thorns. Behind you is a dark shadow which looms ever larger, the spirit of the Fiend from the Pit. It can travel the byways of the ether as easily as you would walk down a flagged road. Your helpless silvery form is blown onward and you cannot stop yourself being impaled on the wall of thorns which protects the Elysian Fields. You are helpless as the Fiend grabs you in its horny embrace, then all goes dark. The terrible ringing of the great bell of Dis, the Iron-city of the Underworld, reverberates around your skull. All around you is cold iron. You have been carried away to hell where you will suffer eternal torment.

303

Aiguchi flails a scything blow at your head but you duck below it and jab up at his exposed throat.

AIGUCHI THE WEAPONMASTER
Defence against Cobra Strike punch: 6
Endurance: 15
Damage: 1 Die + 1

If you have defeated him, turn to **27**. If he is still alive he tries to crack open your skull with a great two-handed blow as you rise to your feet. Your Defence is 7. If you still live, will you use the Cobra Strike punch again (return to the top of this paragraph), the Winged Horse kick (turn to **89**) or the Whirlpool throw (turn to **46**)?

304

Kiyamo and Onikaba are pleased to see you and thank you for ridding the Island of Plenty of one of the ninja of the Way of the Scorpion. You tell Kiyamo of your quest and he says, 'Your destiny is indeed great, Avenger. I will give you a ship to take you to the Mainland,' and he orders that a ship be prepared immediately. He says, 'May Fate smile on you,' and Onikaba and an escort of ten samurai lead you to the port of Lemné. Onikaba turns to you and you thank him before boarding the sloop that awaits you, the '*Sea Dragon*'. The captain asks you where you wish to be taken. Will you travel towards Doomover and thence to Irsmuncast, the more direct route (turn to **330**), or to Tor, where Glaivas, the Ranger-Lord lives and thence to Irsmuncast (turn to **21**)?

305

Honoric falls back past the rhododendrons and a pine tree and you press him hard, until your foot is jerked out from under you and you are hauled upside down into the air. You have stepped in a trapper's snare which was attached by a length of rope to a bent bough of the pine. Now the rope dangles you upside down before Honoric. There is a look of fury in his eyes and Sorcerak smokes inches from your unprotected neck. You prepare to try to block its blow but Honoric is merely staring hard into your eyes. Your gaze is unflinching as you look death in the face but there is not a glimmer of fear in your eye. Honoric speaks, 'I have been cheated by a mere trapper's snare.'

Sorcerak whines through the air and you, momentarily stunned, to the ground. As you shake your head to clear your senses, you see Honoric mount his warhorse and ride off. He has spared your life. Instead of killing you, he cut the rope that held you dangling from the tree. You free yourself from the snare and continue on your way, shaking your head in wonder.

Turn to **13**.

306

'The Spirit Tiger comes,' says the Guardian Angel in sepulchral tones, 'but you may not pass.' The Fiend from the Pit is almost upon you. Will you leave the Gateway to the Seven Heavens, casting yourself once more into the ethereal wind in an effort to escape the clutches of the Fiend (turn to **285**) or try to fight it – perhaps the Guardian Angel will help you (turn to **276**)?

307

The Spectre moves slowly, but if your attack fails its talons will touch you, drawing the life spirit from your body.

SPECTRAL COMPANION
Defence against Iron Fish punch: 7
Endurance: 20

If you win, turn to **327**. If you succeeded in hitting the Spectre you may punch again (return to the top of this paragraph) or use the Leaping Tiger kick (turn to **313**). If you failed the Spectre's talons touch you. If you are carrying a Saint's Locket, turn to **287**. Otherwise turn to **224**.

308

As Onikaba begins his dispositions to attack the barracks, you catch sight of a corpulent figure atop one of the stuccoed villas nearby. It is Golspiel and he is shouting an order to his mercenary captain, Antocidas the One-Eyed. The captain leaves the roof and a minute later appears at the head of a large force of mercenary soldiers, which falls upon Okinaba's men before he can attack. The mob supporting the samurai flees and Onikaba orders his men to retire. They fight fanatically every inch of the way, claiming the lives of many mercenaries. At the last, the mercenaries, afraid of their sharp katana, allow them to make an orderly retreat from the city, but only twenty samurai remain alive. Golspiel has betrayed you. Antocidas now leads his men to the Palace. Turn to **410**.

<h2 style="text-align:center">309</h2>

At last Aiguchi lies dead at your feet. You kneel down beside him and search his body. Amongst his weapons you find a bottle filled with blue liquid labelled 'Waters of Protection from Ethereal Flame'. Note this on your Character Sheet.

Shouldering Aiguchi's body, you take it with you through the Victor's Gate. Beyond the Gate is a small hut. As you approach it, Maak emerges hurriedly, but pulls up with a look of disappointment on his face as he sees who is dead and who still lives. 'I see you triumphed once again,' he says angrily. 'By the laws of the Ring you are now free to go. But once you have left this place you will be fair game for your enemies once more. And you have many enemies, ninja.'

With that he turns on his heel and walks into the hut. You leave the body of Aiguchi outside the hut and run on, heading for Irsmuncast. Turn to **416**.

<h2 style="text-align:center">310</h2>

Leaping up the steps to the throne, you drive your stiffened fingers towards the nerve point beneath the Usurper's ear. The speed of your blow surprises him and you leap back expecting him to fall to the floor. The Usurper's flesh turns red and bloated, swelling unnaturally. Then spikes start to grow out of his back with a noise of tearing flesh. Before your very eyes the Usurper is turning into a Duke of Hell. As you stare, transfixed, he has grown huge bat-like wings, terrible claws and fangs. His face transformed is a mask of hellish evil, far beyond the petty malevolence of mortals. It vents a shriek of anguish and clutches its neck. Your nerve-strike was successful. It has lost 7 from its Endurance of 33.

If you wish to use a nerve-strike again turn to **253**. If you prefer to use your more straightforward martial arts skills, turn to **320**.

311

The figure reins in the charger towering over you as you wait to see what it will do. Will you break the silence and ask it what it is (turn to **237**) or remain silent (turn to **227**)?

312

You inch your way up the Pillar of Death. Just touching it makes your skin crawl, for it seems to pulse slowly with spiritual energy as if it were an ethereal marker on the material plane of Orb. At the top you look around. The view of the ring is excellent from this vantage point. You catch a flash of scarlet from Hunter's Quarry to the north. 'So that is where Aiguchi is hiding!' you think to yourself. Hurriedly climbing down as the menhir becomes more and more disturbing, you move on as quickly as possible into the Duelwood and northwards.

You follow the path until you arrive at the edge of the wood. Ahead of you, gently rolling ground carpeted in long grass leads to a disorganised pile of chalky rocks and boulders lining the rim of Hunter's Quarry. You decide to wait out of sight in the wood, to make sure Aiguchi hasn't moved since you saw him last.

Turn to **190**.

313

The Spectre moves slowly and you summon up all your strength to try to defeat it. If your attack fails, its talons will touch you drawing the life spirit from your body.

SPECTRAL COMPANION
Defence against Leaping Tiger kick: 7
Endurance: 20

If you win, turn to **327**. If you succeeded in hitting the Spectre you may kick again (return to the top of this paragraph) or use the Iron Fist punch (turn to **307**). If you failed and you are carrying a Saint's Locket, turn to **287**. Otherwise, turn to **224**.

As quick as thought, you throw yourself to the ground. Glaivas has done the same, and a crossbow quarrel embeds itself in the ground beside you. Glaivas is on his feet and sprinting around behind the hill immediately. You pick up the bolt and run up the other side of the hill, but meet Glaivas at the summit without having glimpsed your unknown enemy. The crossbow bolt is grooved and there is poison on it. The assassins are at work again. Glaivas suggests once more that you turn north towards the Forest of Arkadan and says that if you wish to travel through the Valley of the Lich-Kings along the highway you can do so without his help. Will you turn north with Glaivas (turn to **111**) or journey on along the road alone (turn to **136**)?

You try to scale the walls of the pit, but you cannot get a good hold in the soft earth. You have no choice but to take the rods of iron from the sleeves of your costume and drive them deep into the walls using them like pitons to climb out of the pit. Eventually you are standing at its top. However, you have been forced to leave the iron rods in the pit. Note that you are unable to block any sharp or metal attacks until you can get some new rods made up. Bright light floods out from the now-opened stone door ahead of you and you step through it to find yourself in a large circular chamber. Immediately before you on the ground is a stone slab, the resting place of a long-dead Lord of Irsmuncast. In the centre of the room stands a marble plinth surrounded by a ring of flames. Upon the plinth rests a thin gold circlet. It is adorned with a single sparkling ruby that glitters in the light. This must be the item you were told would be of use against the Usurper. You cannot discern what the flames are feeding off – indeed there is something very odd about the fire. It gives off a bright white light and the flames flicker and burn about an inch off the ground. The flames are a coppery-yellow and seem insubstantial in some way. Stepping closer you quickly pass your hand through the flame. An agonizing pain fills your soul for an instant, burning at the core of your being.

You realise that these are not physical flames but ethereal flames and that they would not leave your clothes and skin charred and blackened but your very soul itself. Do you have a bottle containing 'Waters of Protection from Ethereal Flame'? If you do, turn to **225**. If you do not, turn to **212**.

316

As Honoric falls back past the rhododendrons and beyond a pine tree, you notice that he has just missed stepping in a snare trap. If you allow him to catch his breath and lure him to attack you again, you judge that he may be caught in the trap. You wait and as he advances the snare tightens round his ankle and a bent bough of the pine tree snaps upright, pulling him off his feet. He hangs upside down before your face, the trapper's snare dangling him from the tree, but he hasn't lost his presence of mind. 'Bear me aloft, Sorcerak,' he shouts, and his body floats out of your reach. He hangs grimly on to the hilt of his sword which pulls him into the topmost leaves of the tree.

A leather pouch falls from his belt, which you scoop up quickly as you hear the sound of many hooves cresting a hill nearby. It is a strong party of Legion of the Sword of Doom. You decide to make good an escape while you can as Honoric blusters furiously, 'You mock me, Fate! It was not destined to end like this.'

But his cries are soon far behind you and his men try to calm him down. You will have to run fast and far to avoid them. Turn to **3**.

You walk away from the tramp at a brisk pace and he hobbles pathetically after you, beseeching you to wait. You quicken your pace back towards the Green and your acute judgment allows you to realise when you look back and see him lit momentarily in a pool of lantern light that he has kept up with you too easily. He is not lame at all. You increase your speed and lose him in a back alley before running on towards the Green and then turning east.

Turn to **269**.

Before you can even move it seems the Guardian Angel has guessed your intention. It speaks a single word, 'Llandymion', and the next thing you know, your mind is pouring itself back into your body. Glaivas starts with relief as he sees you move again, for your body had been absolutely still.

But the whirling of leaves begins again and you have used up your mandrake root. Note that you will not be able to enter the spirit plane again at this time.

Will you launch yourself into a Winged Horse kick at the leaves (turn to **116**) or stand next to Glaivas and wait to see what happens (turn to **128**)?

You tell the old soothsayer you have no gold and her smile becomes a revolting grimace. 'One thing I will tell you gratis, stranger. Take the north road from here and speak to the tramp.' You thank her and leave. Will you take the street that leads north towards the grandiose buildings (turn to **254**) or the street leading east towards the park (turn to **269**)?

'So you dare to challenge Astaroth, seventh Duke of Hell, puny mortal.' The Hell-Duke's flesh burns red and the great leathery wings exude a nauseating stench which causes you to gag. Cursing Fate, who has made it your destiny to fight Astaroth, one of the most powerful denizens of the Nine

Hells, you screw up your courage and give battle. Will you use a kick, either the Winged Horse or Kwon's Flail, if you know it (turn to **267**) or the Tiger's Paw chop (turn to **260**)?

321

You twist aside from his ever-weakening thrusts until they are completely ineffectual, tightening the garrotte all the while. Aiguchi's arms flail feebly and then he is still. You have slain the Weaponmaster. You search the body and amongst his weapons you find two bottles. One is filled with a green liquid and is a Potion of Healing. You may drink it at any time and regain up to 10 points of lost Endurance The other is filled with a blue liquid and is labelled 'Waters of Protection from Ethereal Flame'. Note these on your Character Sheet. Shouldering Aiguchi's body you take it with you through the Victor's Gate. Beyond the Gate is a small hut. As you approach it, Maak emerges hurriedly, but pulls up with a look of disappointment on his face as he sees who is dead and who still lives. 'I see you triumphed once again, ninja,' he says angrily. 'By the laws of the Ring you are now free to go. But once you have left this place you will be fair game for your enemies once more. And you have many enemies, ninja.' With that he turns on his heel and walks into the hut. You leave the body of Aiguchi outside the hut and run on, heading for Irsmuncast. Turn to **416**.

322

At the last moment, Aiguchi senses your presence and spins round as you cry out as the Inner Force leaves you. Your Iron Fist catches him on the shoulder, sending him flying backwards to sprawl on the ground, his face locked in a grimace of pain. You may note that he has lost 10 points from his Endurance of 15. However, he masters himself and rolls away and is onto his feet with great speed, swiftly grabbing his curve-bladed spear or naginata. 'Impressive, ninja,' he grates between gritted teeth. 'You managed that well, but not well enough, for I am a Master of Weapons.' He then executes a mind-boggling series of movements, as if he were fighting several opponents at once. The naginata is almost a blur as he thrusts and parries, performing a complex but deadly dance. You can see that he is very, very fast, but is he as fast as you? Then he begins to edge towards you, crab-like, the tip of his spear always pointed, unerringly, at your throat. You circle each other. Suddenly he hops and thrusts the spear at your belly with great speed, but you sweep it aside with your arm. For a brief moment you are inside the reach of the naginata. If you have the skill of Yubi-Jutsu, you realise he is too quick for you to use a precision nerve-strike, and you will have to slow him down first. Will you try the Leaping Tiger kick (turn to **56**), the Teeth of the Tiger throw (turn to **22**), a Tiger's Paw chop (turn to **38**) or wait for a suitable moment and, using Inner Force, attempt to snap Aiguchi's naginata (turn to **10**)?

323

Slowly, you can feel your mental defences slipping under the psychic onslaught. But you call upon your innermost stores of spiritual energy and find the strength to withstand the Old One. Subtract 1 from your Inner Force. You can sense the surprise and frustrated rage in its mind. Then it redoubles its onslaught. As if from far away, you can see the body of the Old One go rigid with effort. You cry out in pain as it tries to crush your mind. Will you try to hurl a shuriken at the Old One, so as to break its psychic assault (turn to **347**), continue to resist its attack with your mind (turn to **358**) or if you have the skill of Feigning Death, will you sink into a trance, so that the Old One will be unable to reach your mind with its own (turn to **369**)?

324

The figure reins in. Will you hurl a shuriken (turn to **274**), or try to knock it from the saddle with a Leaping Tiger kick from the side (turn to **127**)?

325

Honoric's attack forces you back towards a stand of young pine trees. Sorcerak is everywhere and your sleeve irons are dented and one has sheared clean through. If you have the skill of Picking Locks, Detecting and Disarming Traps, turn to **293**. If not turn to **282**.

326

Your head snaps round towards the hillside just in time to see a crossbow quarrel speeding towards your chest.

If you have the skill of Arrow Cutting, turn to **281**.

If not you can only try your best to knock the quarrel aside with your sleeve guard. Roll for a block as though you were deflecting a blow, treating your Defence against the speeding projectile as 6. If you fail to knock it aside, turn to **272**. If you succeed, turn to **281**.

327

You have defeated the Spectre which turns to flee. Glaivas' scroll seems to have banished one of his foes which turns to dust in moments. He has cast a Raise the Dead spell on the long undead Warlord, whose body suffered the decay of centuries in seconds. The fourth Spectre turns tail and gallops after its fleeing companions. You have fought against members of the Spectral Company and lived.

If you brought Grizell, a slave girl, with you to the canyon mouth, turn to **340**.

If not Glaivas hopes that you will escape the other members of the Company for you would surely die now if found by them. You skirt the mountains, entering the wilderness at dawn. You have travelled through the Valley of the Lich-Rings, from one end to the other. Turn to **299**.

Your training in detecting hidden things alerts you to a thin squarish outline in the side of the Mound where the grass has not grown. You are investigating this area when suddenly it gives way beneath you and you are pitched forward. You fall a yard or two, but somersault safely onto your feet, shielding your head as a shower of earth and pebbles follows you down. Blinking the dust away, you are aware that the small window of light from outside illuminates a low chamber. The air is heavy and stale and the floor is laden with dust. It has been undisturbed for centuries. In the north wall of the chamber a tunnel opening yawns blackly but it is what lies in the centre of the chamber that holds your attention. Upon a low marble slab lies an ancient mummified corpse. Leathery skin, dry as parchment, is drawn tightly over the grinning skull and the body is clothed in once rich and regal robes, now hopelessly decayed. However, a beautiful ivory-handled dagger, etched with a single rune that seems to glow in the dusky light, is buried to the hilt in the centre of the corpse's chest. Two silver torch-holders flank the corpse, still holding two torches burnt out long since. The marble slab is carved to depict scenes showing a single figure repeatedly perpetrating various bloodthirsty and murderous acts. A deathly silence fills the chamber and a shiver runs up your spine. Will you go down the tunnel to the north (turn to **367**) or take the dagger out of the corpse's chest (turn to **356**)?

The Shuriken whistles across the Throne Room and flies to its mark in the Usurper's throat, but the smile never leaves his face. The star falls out of the wound and clatters to the marble floor and the blood that flows is not red, but purplish black. At first it seems as if the Shuriken has done some harm; the Usurper's flesh burns red and bloated. Then spikes start to grow out of his back with a noise of tearing flesh. Before your very eyes the Usurper is turning into a Duke of Hell. As you stare, transfixed, he has grown huge bat-like wings, terrible claws and fangs. His face transformed is a mask of hellish evil, far beyond the petty malevolence of mortals. If you have the skill of Poison Needles you may wish to use one (turn to **336**) or your martial arts skill (turn to **320**).

<h2 style="text-align:center">330</h2>

The journey is an uneventful one and soon the *Sea Dragon* is off the coast of Doomover. Not wishing to enter the city itself, knowing that it is an evil place, where Honoric commands the Legion of the Sword of Doom, you ask the captain to sail near the coast a few miles south of the city. From here you swim to the shore, back in the Manmarch once again. It is growing dark, so you strike inland a little way before camping under a grove of trees for the night. The next morning you rise early and, running lightly, head north-east toward the Barrow Swales and Irsmuncast. Turn to **5**.

<h2 style="text-align:center">331</h2>

As soon as you call a sinuous form takes shape behind the Guardian Angel on the silver road. It is a perfect tiger, but her fur is white and her eyes blue, the Spirit Tiger, servant of Kwon the Redeemer. The Fiend's face creases in feral rage as it realises it has been denied its quarry even at the instant of the kill. The magnificent Spirit Tiger, flawless and powerful, launches herself at the grisly Fiend and a bloody battle begins. The usually calm Spirit Tiger bites and rakes her claws at the Fiend with bestial ferocity although her head is belaboured by crushing blows from the arms of horn. At last the Fiend from the Pit realises that death is about to take it. The horns score deep furrows down the Spirit Tiger's flank but her jaws finally meet in the Fiend's neck. Its grisly form shrivels and is gone. Just its soul like a blackened and shrivelled grub is left to be carried back to the Underworld on the ethereal wind. You are about to offer prayers and thanks to the Spirit Tiger when, far away, the Guardian Angel speaks a single word, 'Llandymion', and you find your mind pouring itself back into your inert body. Glaivas starts with relief as he sees you move again, for your body has been

absolutely still. You tell him what has happened and settle down once more to take what rest you can, free of the feeling of malice that had so darkened your thoughts of late. You rise the next day and continue your journey. Turn to **414**.

332

With a rapid practiced movement, you whip the garrotte around the Weaponmaster's neck. He gives a strangled cry and drops his bow, his hands flying up to his neck. As you tighten your hold, you drive your knee into his back and force him to the ground. Suddenly he has a long dagger in his right hand; desperately he drives it round his back at your ribs with the last of his strength. Roll for a block as you try to avoid the blade whilst keeping your hold on the garrotte, which is now biting into his throat. Your Defence is 5 for this block. If you succeed, turn to **321**. If you fail, turn to **153**.

333

You turn back and crawl quickly along the tunnel you have made through the cornstalks, but Glaivas has gone on. Soon the Palisade of Thorns looms before you and you stand up to climb it and escape. There is a shout behind you and you see that the Halvorcs have followed you, guided by the blackhawk. Glaivas has escaped, but you have the Palisade before you and twenty spear tips behind. If you have the skill of Arrow Cutting, turn to **222**. If not, turn to **203**.

334

The power of your attack has Honoric gasping for breath and be staggers back from you, towards a clump of rhododendron bushes. Determined to allow him no respite, you follow up quickly. If you have the skill of Picking Locks, Detecting and Disarming Traps, turn to **316**. If not, turn to **305**.

335

You struggle desperately but there is nothing you can do, for you are spiritually exhausted. The psychic power of the Old One is simply too much for you and the last thing you hear is the mocking laughter of the creature as your mind is shredded like paper. Soon you are a mindless vegetable, drooling and staring vacantly for the rest of your life, kept alive as a showpiece by the followers of Vile, Nemesis and Vasch-Ro.

336

The cloth-of-gold robes have split and fallen from the massive red torso of the Duke of Hell. The poison needle streaks unseen to its mark in the red flesh, but you see it blacken, smoke and shrivel to nothing. The Duke of Hell advances, towering over you, oblivious to this minor irritation. You will have to use your martial art skills. Turn to **320**.

337

Glaivas replies that if time is so pressing you may as well risk being seen on the road, and so you continue, passing the occasional peasant and a peddler who is so persistent in trying to sell his wares that Glaivas is forced to see him off with the flat of his sword. In the mid-afternoon the road climbs between wooded hills, and Glaivas warns you to be on your guard against ambush. Suddenly there is a metallic click in the bushes above you. Do you turn to look (turn to **326**) or throw yourself to the ground (turn to **314**)?

338

If you have the skill of Yubi-Jutsu, Nerve-Striking, and wish to use it turn to **310**. If not you decide to use a Leaping Tiger kick against the unarmed man – turn to **298**.

339

As you approach the hills you hear the rattle of harness, clink of armour and the snorting of a horse, coming from behind a low ridge. As you watch, a bizarre apparition appears bit by bit above the crest. The sun flashes on the wavy points of a bronzed helmet. As the mount climbs the ridge towards you the whole of the helmet comes into view like a golden sunburst. The front of the gleaming helmet is like an actor's

MYLÈNE VILLENEUVE.COM 2014

mask, with holes for eyes and a narrow curved slit like a sinister smile. It tops a figure clad in elaborate plate armour from head to toe. The horse is a magnificent piebald mare of seventeen hands or so. The figure looks like a metal statue, very still in the saddle. The figure rides down towards you in silence. There is a huge bastard sword strapped across its back, the hilt behind its left shoulder. Do you want to attack now and ask questions later (turn to **324**), stand your ground and wait (turn to **311**) or flee, perhaps wounding the horse if the rider gives chase (turn to **301**)?

340

Grizell is beyond help. The magic from the ranger's scroll is spent and you must leave her frail body to rot. Glaivas hopes that you will escape the other members of the Company for you would surely die now if found by them. You skirt the mountains, entering the wilderness at dawn. You have travelled through the Valley of the Lich-Kings, from one end to the other. Turn to **299**.

341

As the wolf man hurtles towards you, you run to meet it and then jump into the air and somersault over it. It is caught by surprise and you may add 2 to your Attack Modifier for this attack only as it turns to face you. Will you throw a Silver Shuriken or Enchanted Shuriken if you have one (turn to **200**), use the Iron Fist punch (turn to **67**), a Forked Lightning kick (turn to **219**) or a Teeth of the Tiger throw (turn to **364**)?

342

You crawl on, quickly but with stealth, and still the blackhawk's cries taunt you as it circles in the sky. After some time you hear a sound ahead of you. Glaivas stiffens and you both raise your heads to look around. You have been encircled. Ahead of you are ten svart, yellow-eyed Orcs, carrying stabbing swords. Behind and to the sides stand twice as many Halvorcs, their spear-tips pointing towards you above the chest-high corn. You will have to fight your way out. Glaivas' sword whistles from its sheath and, together, you rush to attack the group of Orcs. But before you reach them the blackhawk folds its fourteen-foot wingspan and dives with a light rush of air at your face, cruel talons outstretched. You Defence as you try to block this attack from the sky is 7. If you fail to block, turn to **252**. If you succeed, the blackhawk soars away before you can stop it and the Orcs are upon you. Turn to **241**.

343

'Come! Come, follow,' says the tramp grabbing your arm, and he hobbles down a dark side street. He tells you he used to be a mercenary until he was wounded in the leg by an Orc. If you have the skill of Shin-Ren, turn to **238**. If not read on.

He seems to know that you are a stranger to the city but he doesn't ask you any questions. At last you are outside an inn with a sign-written board above the door – 'The Hostel from the Edge'. You ask the tramp what it means and he tells you that the people of Irsmuncast call the Bowels of Orb, or the Rift, the Edge. Inside is a huge, low vault filled with a hundred or more souls, only about half of whom are human. The balance is formed of Orcs, Halvorcs and a group of dangerous looking Wolfen, erect and arrogant looking. They have the heads of wolves and the bodies of beast-men but they stand over seven feet tall. Peasant girls are carrying tankards to the customers seated at low tables and benches. The tramp shuffles away to get drunk so you decide to find out something about the city. Will you talk to some nearby Halvorcs (turn to **54**) or sit alone and see if you overhear anything of interest (turn to **33**)?

344

You fight against rising panic as you realise the ethereal wind is whirling you further away from your body which stands motionless before the onslaught of the Fiend. You struggle to return to it before it is too late, knowing that if your body is slain your mind will be tossed by the ethereal wind until your soul is washed up on the grey shores of limbo where it will be stranded forever. But you cannot, the wind carries you before it. At last you realise that you have not felt the tug of your wounded body for some time. If you think you are dead, turn to **374**. If you believe you are still alive and wish to continue to struggle, turn to **383**.

345
You find nothing unusual at all. Will you climb the Mound (turn to **300**) leave the Mound and head for the Victor's Gate (turn to **250**) or follow the path north to the crossroads (turn to **273**)?

346
Honoric's concentration is unwavering and he is too old a campaigner to fall for the Dragon's Tail throw. As you slide towards him he leaps back, and Sorcerak's tip slashes your thigh. Pain wracks you – it feels as if the deep wound has filled with acid. You have lost 1 Die + 5 Endurance to the eldritch blade. If you are still alive your lightning reactions save your life as the black blade buries itself deep in the ground where you lay until an instant before. You have rolled aside and you leap to your feet once more as Honoric pulls his blade from the turf. He closes in once more. Will you use the Leaping Tiger kick (turn to **365**) or the Cobra Strike punch (turn to **354**)?

347
You force yourself to reach for a shuriken but the effort is terrible. Make a Fate Roll, applying −2 to your Fate Modifier for this throw only. If you are successful turn to **380**. If you fail, your attempt to throw a shuriken distracted you so that you are unable to maintain your mental defences. Turn to **335**.

348
Making sure there is plenty of distance between yourself and the monster, you scour your surroundings for a suitable place to pray. There is no shrine or temple to Kwon the Redeemer but there is a large cairn of stones on a hilltop nearby. You guess that it may be a shrine made by one of the

ancient hill tribes of the Barrow Swales to the All-Mother, Preserver of Life. Will you climb to the hilltop shrine (turn to **360**), pray where you are in the verdant valley (turn to **372**) or double back on yourself in a wide-arc towards the Temple to Kwon in the city of Mortavalon (turn to **387**)?

349

In the blinking of an eye you send a poison needle through the air with unerring accuracy. It embeds itself in the Usurper's forehead, and he emits a sharp cry of anguish as the poison takes effect. You wait to watch him die in agony, but a hideous transformation takes place. At first it seems the poison is causing his flesh to burn red and bloat, then spikes start to grow out of his back with the noise of tearing flesh. Before your very eyes the Usurper is turning into a Duke of Hell. As you stare, transfixed, he has grown huge, bat-like wings, terrible claws and fangs. His face, transformed, is a mask of hellish evil, far beyond the petty malevolence of mortals. To your amazement you hear it shriek in pain – your poison has hurt it. The Duke of Hell has lost 6 from its Endurance of 33. Will you use another poison needle (turn to **336**) or your martial arts skill (turn to **320**)?

350

You lie dead to the world in the most dangerous region of all Orb. You suffer nightmares once more, the fleshy Golem's hands closing round your throat, but exhaustion overcomes all and you sleep soundly for a day and a night. When at last you reawaken, you are shocked to realise how long you have slept in the steaming desolation at the edge of the yawning darkness of the chasm. Yet you are well: you may restore up to 4 points of lost Endurance for your rest. You stretch then look around. To the west, green and forested hills; to the north, the fissured bleakness of baked mud and black rock that lines the Bowels of Orb. Still feeling drowsy, you set off north-west anxious to leave the chasm behind. There is no telling what evil may issue forth to assail you at any time. Turn to **339**.

When you ask the priests questions concerning the disposition of troops and the timing of their attack they reply that they are experts in timing. 'Are you sure the time is right?' asks one. You reply that feelings run high in the city and that you think this is the time. They nod and indicate, smiling, that they know enough about revolutions to decide for themselves. 'All things come to pass, given time,' says one. Suddenly the conservatory is empty once more and the scribe appears and shows you out. The sun's shadow has moved another hour.

If you wish to approach another faction whom you have not yet spoken to for support, you may approach either the Swordswomen of Dama, Shieldmaiden of the Gods (turn to **296**) or the merchants in their emporia (turn to **184**), or you may try to kindle the rabble (turn to **68**). If you feel you have all the support you need, you make your final preparations to assassinate the Usurper (turn to **9**).

As you approach the immense chasm the vegetation gives way to rocky earth which is blackened and cracked. Pits and fissures scar the ground and noisome fumes rise from the depths of the chasm. The Golem lumbers onwards, its arms outstretched towards you, the rictus grin still splitting its white face. You step to the very edge and it totters onwards, grabbing for your throat, but you leap aside and deliver a Winged Horse kick to its hip. The Golem overbalances and falls into the blackness, but it utters no cry and there is no sound of its body hitting rock below. Perhaps it has fallen to the middle of Orb. Turn to **411**.

As you both break cover the chase is on. Halvorcs, brandishing their spears and bullwhips, trot along breaking down the corn like a pack of wolves following their prey. You can run faster than they but, as the blackhawk wheels through the air and then flies off ahead of you, you decide not to tire yourselves yet, content with simply keeping them at a distance. After a few minutes' hard work running through the corn you espy a group of men and women, chained together and wearing soiled rags, breaking rocks in a fallow field. Orcish overseers chivvy them with slave-lashes. You skirt around them and some of the Orcs take up the chase whilst the slaves stare dully, treating your sudden appearance as no more than a break in the monotonous drudgery of their hopeless lives, for no-one ever escapes from within the Palisade of Thorns. Turn to **264**.

354

Honoric's blade is like a wall of steel as he swipes Sorcerak from side to side in the air. You try to strike below his guard with a lunging jab.

HONORIC
Defence against Cobra Strike punch: 8
Endurance: 24
Damage: 1 Die + 5

If you have reduced Honoric to 12 Endurance or below, turn to **334**. If you hit Honoric and have the skill of Yubi-Jutsu, he loses 11 Endurance, but you may not combine Yubi-Jutsu with Inner Force. If Honoric is not yet seriously wounded you must face his bewitching blade, as Sorcerak whines through the air faster than the eye can follow. Your Defence against the eldritch blade is 7. If you fall to 5 Endurance or below, but are still alive, turn to **325**. Otherwise you may punch again (return to the top of this paragraph), use the Winged Horse kick (turn to **365**) or the Dragon's Tail throw (turn to **346**).

355

It is a glorious and sunny morning, the first day of Demondim, when you set out with Glaivas the Ranger from the city of Tor. Glaivas has done much to prepare those people of his city who might be relied upon to fight against evil, should Honoric lead the Legion the Sword of Doom to war, but he believes it is safe to leave the city for the month

of Demondim. He has recently survived an attempt on his life by the Assassin's Guild and he has heard that one Mandrake, Guildmaster of Assassins in far-away Wargrave Abbas, has spread the word that he is interested in your whereabouts. Glaivas suggests that you leave the well-trodden paths of the many towns and villages around Tor behind and strike out north towards the deep forests of Arkadan. If you agree, turn to **111**. If you argue that you would like to make quicker progress by using the roads, turn to **337**.

356

You approach the marble slab. Slowly you reach out and close your fingers around the hilt. As you tug it comes free. A chill breath of wind seems to fill the chamber. Then, as you secretly expected, the corpse's eyelids flicker open, revealing two burning red coals, rooting you to the spot with fear. Suddenly its skeletal hand whips out and fastens onto your throat, the wicked talons digging into your windpipe. You gasp in pain and shock as the fingers begin to constrict. Lose 2 Endurance.

The pain galvanises you into action. Will you chop down at the creature's wrist with a Tiger's Paw chop, to break its hold (turn to **382**), plunge the dagger back into its chest (turn to **398**) or try and use your flint and tinder to set its clothes alight (turn to **210**)?

357

The journey to the mountains takes days. You swim the river Greenblood and the monster walks across the river-bed, as it cannot be drowned. Next you cross the road that runs from the Spires of Foreshadowing to the university city of Greyguilds-on-the-Moor. You dare not stop to sleep but rest with your eyes open, staring in the direction of the pursuing Golem. Only your iron hardness makes it possible to continue, though your titanic strength of will is sorely tested. At last you enter the foothills of the Horn Mountains and make for a tall peak. If you have the skill of Climbing, turn to **151**. If you do not have this skill you will be in the lap of Fate as you attempt the climb. Will you take the risk and attempt it (turn to **142**) or turn east and then north again, towards the forested hills (turn to **97**)?

358

If you have no Inner Force left, turn to **335**. If you have, read on. You can feel the Old One's mental grasp tightening horribly, causing you to gasp with pain and effort. Somehow you manage to call upon further reserves of energy. Subtract 1 from your Inner Force again. A few moments of almost unendurable agony pass by and then, abruptly, the mental assault ceases. You stagger with the sudden release, weak and dizzy, but you soon regain control of yourself. The Old One backs away from you and says 'You are remarkably strong, Avenger, stronger than I had thought possible, but can you withstand this?' With that he passes his tentacled hand through the air in a series of complicated gestures. Suddenly, before your very eyes, an exact replica of yourself materialises, dressed as you. You gape in astonishment but recover quickly as you see yourself assuming a position in the Way of the Tiger as if readying to kick. The Old One stands behind your double in silent concentration. Will you attack your duplicate (turn to **408**) or calmly try to walk straight through your double and attack the Old One (turn to **400**)?

359

The woman's face looks stern and preoccupied in the lamplight. Will you ask her the way to the Temple to Kwon (turn to **292**) or let her pass by and seek an inn where you may find out more about the mood of the populace (turn to **401**)?

360

You break the skyline at the top of the hill and the view is breathtaking and beautiful. To the south beyond the lower hills is the valley of the river Greenblood. To the north is a wilderness of trees and meadows. The cairn has been raised ten feet above the ground and you clamber to its top and commend yourself in prayer to the All-Mother, Preserver of Life. Will you crave her help as one who intends to bring the rule of Law and Good to the city of Irsmuncast (turn to **371**) or pray as one who seeks aid against an unnatural monster that is an abomination, not a living being (turn to **391**)?

361

As the silk flag flutters down to the tower roof you walk to the battlements and look out over the panorama of the city. You can clearly see Force-Lady Gwyneth on a grey warhorse, apparently inspecting her troops. They are ranged in serried ranks on the parade ground beyond Cross Street. The majority are women, but a sizeable number of men, too, carry the lozenge-shaped shields of Dama. A few are in full plate armour, their faces hidden behind visors. A small detachment of Halvorcs and men bearing the Usurper's stag emblem slouch nearby, at ease. Gwyneth's lieutenant points up at you and the trumpeter sounds five short notes. Gwyneth shouts a command and the shieldmaidens divide into two, half marching towards the Palace and half towards the army barracks.

The detachment of Halvorcs and men react slowly – many have fallen to quick sword thrusts before they realise that the revolt has begun. Then they flee. The skill at arms of Gwyneth's warriors is a joy to behold as they meet the Usurper's men in open battle on the streets below. They are reinforced by the monks of Kwon and for some time the fighting sways back and forth, but the warrior-women are outnumbered and their advance is halted before the Palace gates. Looking down to Cross Street you can see that the barracks is holding out and a group of priests are leaving the Temple to Nemesis, marching to the relief of the army. The battle hangs in the balance. There is nothing you can do but watch. It would be foolish to fight your way out through the Palace.

Suddenly, as if from nowhere, a horde of people appear around the priests of Nemesis. The mob has risen, arming themselves with short swords, axes and clubs. The spells of the priests kill many of the crowd but they are forced to retire inside the Temple. The word spreads like wildfire through the city and the streets become thronged with people. The army is forced to give way and the shieldmaidens and monks gain the walls of the Palace garden.

If the Shogun Kiyamo of the Island of Plenty gave you a hundred samurai under the command of Onikaba, and you ordered them to journey to Doomover and across the Manmarch, rather than through the Valley of the Lich-Kings, turn to **375**. Otherwise it is only a matter of time before the Usurper's army must surrender: turn to **420**.

362

She takes the payment and then caresses the crystal ball. 'This sphere of foretelling links me to the Oracle of Oracles, Terengedion. I see you are a traveller, from afar, but you have never travelled to Terengedion, near the jungle of Khesh. I see much, you come from beyond the Endless Sea, but your future is uncertain, stranger. Violence surrounds you – you have the look of Death!'

She stiffens then crouches even lower over the great glass orb but you can see nothing within it. 'I cannot foretell your future. Your destiny hangs in the balance,' and she places a dark cloth over the crystal ball. Fortune tellers never tell their clients of their own imminent death you muse, but you are, in a way, grateful for the uncertainty.

'At least tell me which road I shall take from the Green.'

'Your way lies east,' she replies. You experience a chill of morbid superstition and decide to leave. Will you take the street leading north towards the grandiose buildings (turn to **254**) or east towards the park (turn to **269**)?

363

The Throne Room is decorated with the insignia of the Usurper, but you can see the hippogriff and chequerboard coat of arms behind the throne and a statue of a warrior-woman, or the goddess Dama, beyond it. Sitting on the carven throne is the Usurper. You have never before seen his likeness, but the cold eyes and cruel yet handsome face could only be those of a tyrant. He is dressed in cloth-of-gold which shimmers as he moves and he bears the golden rose-crown of the Overlords of Irsmuncast on his brow. Although you have made no sound, he senses you, turning his head to look as you leap into the Throne Room. He is alone and unarmed. The doors are shut and there are no guards within; all you have to do is kill him and the people of Irsmuncast will be free of the yoke of his oppression. You reach for a shuriken, intending to rip his throat out before he can call for help, but he merely smiles and beckons you to him. You become suspicious and reconsider your move. If you have the skill of Poison Needles and wish to use one, turn to **349**. If you wish to attack the unarmed Usurper using martial arts combat, turn to **338**. If you have a Silver Shuriken or Enchanted Shuriken and wish to use it, turn to **329**.

364

As the creature gathers itself for a leap at your throat, you jump and try to lock your legs around its neck and twist savagely.

WEREWOLF
Defence against Teeth of the Tiger throw: 7
Endurance: 14
Damage: 1 Die + 2

If you have successfully thrown him, you may punch (turn to **67**) or kick (turn to **219**) the creature as it struggles on its back briefly, adding 2 to your Punch or Kick Modifier and damage for this attack only. If you failed to throw the Werewolf, its snapping jaws lunge for your throat as you come back onto your feet. Your Defence is 6. If you are still alive, will you use the Iron Fist punch (turn to **67**) or the Forked Lightning kick (turn to **219**)?

365

Sorcerak's tip shadows your every move as you make your feint, then lash out with a Leaping Tiger kick at Honoric's head.

HONORIC
Defence against Leaping Tiger kick: 9
Endurance: 24
Damage: 1 Die + 5

If you have reduced Honoric to 12 Endurance or below, turn to **334**. If you hit Honoric and have the skill of Yubi-Jutsu, he loses 11 Endurance, but you may not combine Yubi-Jutsu with Inner Force. If Honoric is not yet seriously wounded you must face his bewitching blade as Sorcerak whines through the air faster than the eye can follow. Your Defence against the eldritch blade is 7. If you fall to 5 Endurance or below, but are still alive, turn to **325**. Otherwise you may kick again (return to the top of this paragraph), use the Cobra Strike punch (turn to **354**) or the Dragon's Tail throw (turn to **346**).

366

You stand up and send a throwing star skywards with a single fluid movement. It sparkles in the sun but the blackhawk is too high and the shuriken falls harmlessly to the ground, lost in the corn. There is a shout to your right and you turn to see a band of twenty or so Halvorcs, crossbreeds as tall as men but with orcish features. They are dressed in brown leather armour and carry spears and bullwhips. Glaivas curses you for a fool and calls you to follow him, before setting off to the north-east at a run, and you follow (turn to **353**).

367

You walk into the dark tunnel. It goes down a little and then levels off. After a while you see a small patch of daylight up ahead. Drawing closer, you can make out a small opening, just large enough for you to crawl through. Looking out, you can see a jumble of stones and boulders in a large roughly circular pit. You realise the tunnel comes out inside Hunter's Quarry. Looking up and to the left at the rim of the quarry, the sight that greets you causes you to stiffen in surprise. Aiguchi is crouched behind a large boulder at the top of the quarry, his back to you. He is concentrating on watching something, presumably the wood, hoping to catch you unawares in the open with his bow. You crawl out into the quarry without alerting him. He is about twenty feet away from you.

Will you try and spit a poison needle, if you have the skill of Poison Needles, although he is at extreme range (turn to **148**), try to creep up behind him (turn to **173**), or hurl a shuriken at him (turn to **415**)?

<h2 style="text-align:center">368</h2>

Glaivas agrees that you stand the least chance of being discovered if you travel to Irsmuncast along the river Greybones before turning north, but cautions you that the dangers are so great that you might never live to see that city at all. It is plain that he has suffered some personal hurt which has to do with that part of Orb called the Valley of the Lich-Kings, but what he tells you of it is enough to explain his reticence on the *Aquamarin*. As he speaks the sky darkens and it begins to rain heavily, the water drumming on the roof slates. His face looks pale in the gloom as he tells you that two beings calling themselves immortals rule over that valley. Each keeps his own court, one in the Walls of Shadow, a city whose walls always shed an unnatural darkness beneath them, no matter how bright the sun, and the City of the Runes of Doom. He mutters a prayer to the All-Mother as he speaks the name. The City of the Runes of Doom lies on the banks of the Greybones itself, and for more than a millennium its tyrannical ruler has been the Fleshless King, a necromancer who discovered the awful secrets of half-life after death, a skeletal being kept alive only by the power of his arcane magicks and the daily sacrifice of a virgin to his god, Death. The people of the city are fed by slaves, men and women forced to till the fields by cruel orcish overseers, and the walls of the great cathedral of Death are dyed the purple of putrefying flesh. Glaivas says that he will guide you through the Valley of the Lich-Kings and you set out together in the morning.

Turn to **355**.

You sink to your knees, calming your body and slowing your heart rate, your mind slipping from the mental grasp of the Old One, like a fish slithering from the hands of the fisherman back into the sea. Soon you are in the meditative trance of the ninja of the Island of Tranquil Dreams, your mind far from psychic assaults, out of reach of the mental power of the Old One. A few seconds later, you feel, as if from a great, great distance a sharp pain in your face. Quickly you surge back into consciousness and a horrific visage fills your eyes. The Old One has the tentacles around its mouth wrapped around your head, the mouth trying to gnaw at you. Its tentacles seem to be secreting some acidic substance that is eating into your skin agonisingly, as if it were digesting you. Lose 2 Endurance. If you are still alive, you drive a Cobra Strike punch up into its midriff. The effect is instantaneous. The Old One leaps back, doubled up in pain. 'You are a powerful adversary, ninja, with many talents,' it grates. 'I have underestimated you. But can you withstand this?' With that he passes his tentacled hand through the air in a series of complicated gestures. Suddenly, before your very eyes, an exact replica of yourself materialises, dressed as you. You gape in astonishment but recover quickly as you see yourself assuming a position in the Way of the Tiger as if readying to kick. The Old One stands behind your double in silent concentration. Will you attack your duplicate (turn to **408**) or calmly try to walk straight through your double and attack the Old One (turn to **400**)?

As the silk flag flutters down to the tower roof you walk to the battlements and look out over the panorama of the city. For a while nothing happens. Has the Demagogue betrayed you, you wonder? But then the streets begin to fill with people appearing as if from nowhere. The mob has arisen, armed with clubs, axes and short swords. They swirl in a disordered mass towards the Palace, where the Usurper's army stands their ground to repulse them.

The army pours out of the barracks to help the Palace

guard but they are attacked from every side street and their progress is slow but steady. The monks of Kwon join in the attack against the Palace, striking down many of the soldiers with their bare fists. The piles of dead form great barriers between the combatants. The Usurper's men are far outnumbered but their superior skills, weapons and armour afford a great advantage. If the mob does not win through soon, you guess that their morale will break in the face of such heavy losses. Only their hatred of the Usurper drives them on. There is nothing you can do but watch. It would be foolish to fight your way out through the Palace.

If the Shogun Kiyamo of the Island of Plenty gave you a hundred samurai under the orders of Onikaba, and you ordered them to journey to Doomover and across the Manmarch, turn to **399**. If he did not, or if you ordered them through the Valley of the Lich-Kings, turn to **410**.

371

Your prayer to the All-Mother will be your last. She holds to the balance of nature and sees Law, Goodness, Evil and Chaos as an interference with the natural scheme of things. A coruscating flash of lightning cracks across the blue sky and strikes the cairn. You are turned to unidentifiable remains of charred flesh. Even the Golem can see that you are dead.

372

You kneel and raise your arms in supplication. Will you pray to Kwon the Redeemer (turn to **385**) or to one of his servants (turn to **392**)?

373

His evil sword radiates an aura of fear that makes moving against him difficult. If you have the skill of Shin-Ren, you can use your Training of the Heart to banish the fear. If not, all your Modifiers are reduced by 1 during this battle.

Honoric is content to rely upon his speed to meet your best move, as you circle him warily. He is also content to let the first move be yours, staring at you over the shield which bears the pendant sword of doom, silver on black. The haughtiness has left his face to be replaced by the alert look of complete concentration that marks a professional swordsman. Will you try to get past his guard by feigning a punch then using the Leaping Tiger kick (turn to **365**), lunge low with the Cobra Strike punch (turn to **354**) or use the Dragon's Tail throw (turn to **346**)?

374
As you become certain that all life has been beaten out of your body, your spirit floats freely in the ethereal wind. You are blown this way and that, seemingly at random, until a gleaming archway shimmers before you, a silver pathway beyond it stretching up into the white clouds. Behind you a dark cloud gathers and takes the shape of the Fiend from the Pit. It travels the byways of the ether as easily as you would walk down a flagged road. Two cherubs fly towards you and lead you to the archway where the Guardian Angel stands as a sentinel, guarding the entrance to the Seven Heavens. The Guardian Angel bars your way, saying, 'Your body breathes yet, you may not pass.' Its expression becomes grim as the Fiend looms behind you. It wails like a banshee and the cherubs flee up the silver pathway beating their gossamer wings in panic, but the sentinel stands firm as the Fiend cries, 'If I complete my task, robbing your body of life, your spirit shall gain eternal repose in Heaven. I had far rather you earned it. I give you your life; you may still waver from the straight and narrow path.' With that it is gone. The Guardian Angel speaks one word 'Llandymion', and before you realise what has happened your mind is flowing back into your body, which is sorely hurt. You have 3 Endurance left. Turn to **18**.

375
To your amazement Onikaba appears at the head of a hundred samurai, resplendent in red lacquered armour. They advance up Palace Road towards the Palace and the sight of this formidable band breaks the morale of the defenders utterly. Turn to **420**.

You glide soundlessly up to his back and he is still not aware of your presence. Will you take out your garrotte and strangle him (turn to **332**), use Inner Force, if you have any left, and drive an Iron Fist punch at the back of his head (turn to **322**) or if you have the skill of Yubi-Jutsu, drive your fist in a nerve-strike at the back of his neck (turn to **406**)?

The tramp accepts the money fawningly and then hobbles back towards the Green, holding onto your arm. He tells you he used to be a mercenary until he was wounded in the leg by an Orc. If you have the skill of Shin-Ren, turn to **238**. He seems to know that you are a stranger to the city and asks out of the blue which is your own Temple to Kwon. Will you tell him the truth (turn to **205**) or say that you are from the city of Mortavalon which also boasts a Temple to Kwon (turn to **186**)?

As the silk flag flutters down to the tower roof you walk to the battlements and look out over the panorama of the city. All is as usual, people going about their daily business, harassed occasionally by the Usurper's soldiers. There is no revolution; a few people notice that the flag has fallen but they merely point and look. The sounds of many footsteps on the staircase of the tower reach you; your revolution has not even begun and you are trapped like a cur on the tower roof. Too tired to resist for long you are taken to be tortured. Wishing to cheat your captors of their pleasure you bite your tongue from your own mouth, expecting to bleed to death, but a sadistic priest of Nemesis casts a spell of healing which closes the wound. You are to be broken on the wheel within sight of the Temple to Kwon.

The hours stretch into days as you traverse the miles to the east. Leaving the Spires of Foreshadowing far behind, you bypass also the university city of Greyguilds-on-the-Moor, and push yourself ever forward. You dare not stop to sleep but rest with your eyes open, staring in the direction of the pursuing Golem. Your breaking point draws near. Then, in an encroaching dusk, you see tall black cliffs in the distance. Turn to **352**.

380

Your mental defences are beginning to slip. The agony is terrible but you make a superhuman effort, screaming as you do so. You manage to send a shuriken spinning towards the Old One. It strikes home and abruptly the mental assault ceases. You stagger for a moment. The Old One hisses in pain, the shuriken embedded in its arm. Quickly you prepare to attack it, but the creature hurriedly steps back and then passes its tentacled hand through the air in a series of complicated gestures. Suddenly, an exact replica of yourself materialises before you, dressed as you. You gape in astonishment but recover quickly as you see yourself assuming a position in the Way of the Tiger as if it were readying itself to kick you. The Old One stands behind your double in silent concentration. Will you attack your duplicate (turn to **408**) or calmly try to walk straight through your double and attack the Old One (turn to **400**)?

381

Glaivas is bidding farewell to a woman of perhaps a hundred seasons. She is short-haired but her face is made up with rouge to look like a doll, or perhaps a small child. Your eyebrows rise in surprise, but then you realise that she is a priestess of Time in the guise of the Youngest Son. You step aside from the path and she bows then sweeps out into the street. Glaivas smiles and beckons but does not greet you by name until you are seated before a peat-fire in his parlour. You tell him of your unlooked-for new mission and he tells you, in return, what he knew of your father.

'He was not a man who sought greatness,' he says, 'but one who suffered greatness to be thrust upon him for the common good. He was a wise and popular ruler, enlightened

but no despot. Many in Irsmuncast still grieve for him.' When he has told you all he knows of your father, the Loremaster, you say. 'I asked you once, on your fair ship the *Aquamarin*, of the cities which lie beyond Tor on the Greybones river, but you would not speak of them. I ask you again, only because I have chosen that course to approach the city of Irsmuncast without exciting suspicion.'

Glaivas sighs heavily and then asks you into his study, where a large bureau is full of valuable scroll-maps. He pins several out on a felt-topped table showing you new lands of which you have never heard. One shows a new continent named the Lands of No Return, another the Forest of Fables, another shows the islands beyond the clashing rocks called the Fangs of Nadir and yet another, Southern Lands. Glaivas gifts you another finely-crafted map showing the Greybones river, the Manmarch and Beyond the Rift. Glaivas goes on to ask you which way you plan to travel.

Turn to **368**.

382

You drive the side of your hand, hardened by years of training, at the thing's bony wrist, but incredibly the ancient bones hold and your attack has only caused the corpse's talons to wrench painfully at your neck. The grip tightens and you begin to struggle for breath. Lose 3 Endurance. If you are still alive you will have to try something else. Will you plunge the dagger back into the corpse's chest (turn to **398**) or try and use your flint and tinder to set its clothes alight (turn to **210**)?

383

In the hope that there is still breath in your body, you bend your will to try to return to it. At last you are succeeding when a dark cloud gathers before you. It becomes the Fiend from the Pit, who can travel the byways of the ether as easily as you would walk down a flagged road. You are helpless as it seizes you in a horny embrace, then all goes dark. The terrible ringing of the great bell of Dis, the Iron-city of the Underworld, reverberates around your skull. All around you is cold iron. You have been carried away to hell where you will suffer eternal torment.

384

Sorcerak leaves its sheath with a snake-like hiss and your heart palpitates with fear at the sight of the rune-covered blacksteel blade. When Honoric is almost within sword-range you blow a poison needle which buries itself in his lip, just below his bristling moustache. He staggers back, his face a mask of pain, but you remember, too late, that he has already survived even the Blood of Nil and the poison has little effect. He advances upon you again, Sorcerak's black blade smoking evilly. Turn to **373**.

385

You pray to your god, but the balmy air remains still and oppressive. Your heartfelt prayers are answered with silence. Either Kwon cannot hear you or he is unable to answer you, perhaps due to the influence of other gods. Will you climb to the hilltop shrine (turn to **360**), double back on yourself in a wide arc towards the Temple to Kwon in the city of Mortavalon (turn to **387**) or head south to the Mountains of Horn, hoping that the monster will fall to its destruction there (turn to **357**)?

386

'We may look old to you, young warrior, and indeed we are, even by the reckoning of the very old, but we are steeped in the thaumaturgical arts', says the tallest of the three and he speaks another word which you do not catch. Suddenly you are alone in the conservatory. Seconds later, the side door opens again and the same three priests file in. The sense of *déja vu* is overwhelming. The one who spoke points out of the window. The sun is low in the sky and the shadow cast by the Temple's spire on the courtyard sundial shows that two hours have passed in what seemed to you an instant. These priests can actually stop time. This is powerful magic. Indeed, they could have killed you without your knowing, even a child could have.

You find yourself gushing praise, quite overwhelmed with what has happened, then, checking yourself, you ask if you can count on the Temple's support. The same priest who cast the spell says, 'Yes, young one, you can.' You tell them that the lowering of the Usurper's flag will mean that you have killed him and that this is the signal for them to act. You assure them that they will not lose any privileges under your rule.

If you are satisfied, you may leave the Temple, return to the Temple to Kwon and arrange with the High Grandmaster to approach a faction who you have not yet spoken to for support. You can approach either the Swordswomen of Dama, Shieldmaiden of the Gods (turn to **296**) or the merchants in their emporia (turn to **184**), or you may try to kindle the rabble (turn to **68**).

If you feel you have all the support you need, you make your final preparations to assassinate the Usurper (turn to **9**).

If you wish to press the three priests as to what they will actually do when the flag comes down, turn to **351**.

387

As you double back in a wide arc, the misshapen mountain of flesh that is the Golem strides to cut you off, its legs pounding relentlessly like a juggernaut. You haven't the strength left to outdistance it.

Will you pause and give battle once more (turn to **259**), climb to the hilltop shrine (turn to **360**) or head south to the Mountains of Horn, hoping that the monster will fall to its destruction there (turn to **357**)?

388

Once you have made sure that Doré le Jeune will not die you move to leave the Throne Room. Doré asks you what lies beyond this room, pointing to the dungeons; you tell him, warning of the Cave Trolls. 'Cave Trolls!' he cries and heads determinedly in their direction. Wondering whether you will ever see him again you turn to the task at hand once more. Turn to **189**.

You are ten feet away from him when he senses your presence and spins round to face you, a look of surprise on his face that soon changes to anger.

'Impressive, ninja. You did well to get so far,' he rasps through gritted teeth. 'But not good enough, for I am a Master of Weapons!' and he throws down his bow and quiver and picks up his curve-bladed spear, the naginata.

He executes a mind-boggling series of movements, as if he were fighting several opponents at once. The naginata is almost a blur as he thrusts and parries, performing a complex but deadly dance. You can see that he is very, very fast, but is he as fast as you?

He begins to edge towards you, crab-like, the tip of his spear always pointed, unerringly, at your throat. You circle each other. Suddenly he hops and thrusts the spear at your belly with great speed, but you sweep it aside with your arm. For a brief moment you are inside the reach of the naginata. If you have the skill of Yubi-Jutsu, you realise he is too quick for you to use a precision nerve-strike, and you will have to slow him down first. Will you try the Leaping Tiger kick (turn to **56**), the Teeth of the Tiger throw (turn to **22**), a Tiger's Paw chop (turn to **38**) or wait for a suitable moment and, using Inner Force, attempt to snap Aiguchi's naginata (turn to **10**)?

You have beaten yourself. As the body of your double falls to the floor it disappears. At this the Old One traces a rectangle in the air with its hand, which leaves a glowing reddish trail of mystic energy behind. Suddenly the rectangle fills with blackness as black as night and the Old One steps in, the magical doorway closing up behind it leaving you alone in the small chamber.

You stare for a moment, astonished at what you have just witnessed, but soon you are back to the business in hand. Searching the chamber, you find that all the scrolls and books are in some script you have no knowledge of, nor do you find anything else of interest, save for a loose torch bracket in one wall. You pull at it and it clicks down. Then a section of the wall swings open, revealing the Throne Room of the Overlord of Irsmuncast. Turn to **363**.

391
You cannot tell whether your prayer has been answered, but a sudden insight sparks in your mind and a plan forms. If you lead the Golem to the Bowels of Orb, the Rift which leads to the centre of Orb and from which much of the evil of the world comes forth, and somehow topple the Golem into that chasm, then will the enchantment which forces it to try to kill you be broken. Then there is silence. You send up a prayer of thanks to the All-Mother and rise to your feet once more in time to hear the thud, thud of the monster's footsteps as it approaches. Will you lead it to the Bowels of Orb (turn to **379**) or turn south hoping that it will fall to its destruction trying to climb after you up one of the peaks (turn to **357**)?

392
Make a Fate Roll. If Fate smiles on you, turn to **409**. If Fate turns her back on you, turn to **413**.

393
The people of Tor seem untroubled by events in the Manmarch and business is as thriving as ever. Soon you are nearing the end of Temple Street and you push open the wrought-iron gate that surrounds a beautiful but wayward looking garden, a haven of nature in the busy city. Glaivas comes to the doorway. Turn to **381**.

394
You tell the High Grandmaster that you intend to approach the priests of Time and he says that he will arrange for a meeting between you and the heads of their temple.

Later that day, you walk down a wide road called the Avenue of Seasons towards a large temple which seems to consist of a single silver dome, rising like a flower bulb into a tall spire which acts as a sundial on the wide square to the

south of the temple. The symbols of a budding shoot, an open flower, a yellow leaf and a pile of dust dominate the temple front. Above the gate are the words 'Time the Snowfather – Eldest Father – Youngest Son – from whose touch none is immune, without whom we would neither be nor die'. You give a password at the temple gate and are ushered into a sunny conservatory by a scribe. A grey statue of an aged but wise man with his hands on the shoulders of a very young but precocious-looking boy dominates the sunny room.

A side door opens and three priests enter, each in his way resembling the old man of the statue, each clad in grey robes with white belts. As you look into their rheumy eyes, you feel that it would be difficult to lie to them. Taking the bit between your teeth you show them your father's hippogriff seal and tell them who you are. They seem to believe you and one of them remarks that your father was a wise man who did much to help the poor so you reply that, with their help, you will do the same, if only the Usurper's forces can be beaten. You ask them what power they might wield if it came to a revolution.

Turn to **386**.

395

As Onikaba begins his dispositions to attack the barracks, you catch sight of a corpulent figure atop one of the stuccoed villas nearby. It can only be Golspiel of the Silver Tongue, spokesman of the merchants of Irsmuncast, and he is shouting an order to his mercenary captain, Antocidas the One-Eyed.

The captain leaves the roof and a minute later appears at the head of a large force of mercenary soldiers, which joins forces with Onikaba's men. The mob joins in on a great attack on the barracks and the Usurper's army surrenders, before all its men are butchered. The word spreads like wildfire and the streets are filled with a howling mob which surges towards the Palace.

Turn to **420**.

396

As you roll over slowly on the pine needles, Glaivas' sword strikes the Fiend in the back, but it seems to make no impression on the monster and he too is wounded. The Fiend towers over you once more. It scoops you up and then buries its horn-tipped arms into your sides. Lose 7 Endurance. If you are still alive you hear Glaivas shouting, 'Sing, sing a song of gladness against the magic.' Turn to **418**.

397

Sorcerak leaves its sheath with a snake-like hiss as, with the speed of a mongoose, you send a glittering throwing star whizzing through the air. With a deftness that is surprising in one of his bulk, Honoric brings up the smoking blade of his sword to knock aside your star. Your heart palpitates with fear at the sight of the rune-carved blacksteel blade. There is no ring of steel on steel, instead the shuriken arcs upward in the sky, spinning away to land harmlessly far behind him. You will be unable to retrieve it.

Honoric laughs, crying, 'Your god has deserted you, Avenger. Kwon, the god of those who fear the sword, will not help you against the chosen general of the war god.' With that he advances upon you, Sorcerak's black blade smoking evilly in the balmy air. You have no time to wonder whether his words are true, as you fight a wave of fear from the eldritch blade.

Turn to **373**.

398

You raise the dagger and plunge it into the living corpse's chest. There is a rasping thud as it bites home. The rune on the dagger flares brightly, momentarily blinding you, and the corpse shudders. The hand fastened on your neck loosens and drops to its side. The glowing red eyes begin to dim and then to fade out completely. It lies inert once more. You stagger back, gasping for breath. When you have recovered and calmed yourself, you decide it would be best to leave the dagger where it is and go down the tunnel. Turn to **367**.

To your amazement you can see an orderly group of warriors, resplendent in red lacquered armour advancing across the Green and northwards towards the Palace. They attract a following of people which swells around them as they approach the Palace, then Onikaba orders them west, against the army barracks. If you have a Jade Lotus blossom, a token from Golspiel the merchant, turn to **308**. If you do not, turn to **395**.

Telling yourself it is but an illusion, you walk straight at your double. Just as you are about to strike it, it disappears! You realise it was an illusion after all, an illusion projected into your own mind and by disbelieving it, you were able to banish it from your sight. At this the Old One traces a rectangle in the air with its hand, which leaves a glowing reddish trail of mystic energy behind. Suddenly the rectangle fills with blackness as black as night and the Old One steps in, the magical doorway closing up behind it leaving you alone in the small chamber.

You stare for a moment astonished at what you have just witnessed but soon you are back to the business in hand. Searching the chamber, you find that all the scrolls and books are in some script you have no knowledge of, nor do you find anything else of interest, save for a loose torch bracket in one wall. You pull at it and it clicks down. Then a section of the wall swings open, revealing the Throne Room of the Overlord of Irsmuncast.

Turn to **363**.

You walk down a dark side street heading east and cross all the way to the far eastern wall of the city. Wandering, you catch sight of the door to an inn with a sign-written board above it saying, 'The Hostel from the Edge'. Inside is a huge, low vault filled with a hundred or more souls, only half of whom are human. The balance is formed of Orcs and Halvorcs. Peasant girls are carrying tankards to the customers, seated at low tables and benches. You are lucky to overhear some Orcs talking with relish of the breaking on the wheel of two innocent scapegoats above the gates to the park, in full view of the Temple to Kwon. Hearing this you decide to slip out of the inn and back to the Green and then turn east again to find the temple.

Turn to **269**.

402

Using your power of mind over matter, you force yourself to ignore the Fiend and relax utterly. The root has freed your mind from the ties of belief which bind it to your body and it floats gently upwards. You can see the top of Glaivas' head and the outspread wings of the Fiend, and your own body, slumped motionless behind the tree. Glaivas buries his sword in the monster's wing but it seems to have no effect. Instead the Fiend stalks around the tree, towering over your motionless body. It raises its great club-horned arms ready to beat your torso to a pulp. Suddenly the ethereal wind rushes your spirit far away but you feel the pull of your body as it suffers the first attack of the Fiend. You lose 8 Endurance as the horns batter your rib-cage. Regardless of your Endurance remaining, even if it is 0 or less, turn to **344**.

403

The Grandmaster of the Dawn taught you Training of the Heart so well that you can hear the duplicity even in the guileful Golspiel's voice. You can be reasonably certain that he is going to betray you and so you decide to tell him that you know of this but will spare his life if he changes his mind. He says nothing of your ultimatum, but gives you an Amber Pendant as a 'token of respect'. Note it on your Character Sheet. You can tell that he has decided not to betray you, but there is no hope for cooperation on any other agreement, and so you leave.

If you wish to approach another faction with whom you have not yet spoken, will it be the Swordswomen of Dama, Shieldmaiden of the Gods (turn to **296**), the priesthood of the Temple to Time (turn to **394**) or the rabble of the city (turn to **68**)? If you feel you have the support you need, you make your final preparations to assassinate the Usurper (turn to **9**).

You wade the river and carefully climb the hill. The outside of the Palisade has not been trimmed and you are able to clamber to the top without being pricked by any of its poisonous thorns, then leap to the corn field beyond. The inside of the hedge is newly cut and overhangs; it is designed not to keep people out, but to keep them in. There are mud-brick guard huts at intervals around the perimeter to either side and you both drop to your bellies to worm your way through the ripening corn which grows so close that you cannot avoid leaving a narrow tunnel of flattened straw behind you. A blackhawk's cry startles you and you look up to see the great bird circling above you, before veering away ahead of you and to the right.

Glaivas hopes that it may have been just a wild bird and you continue to worm your way stealthily through the corn, but before long the blackhawk returns to circle high above you, crying loudly. Will you try to silence it with a shuriken (turn to **366**), get up and run (turn to **353**), continue to crawl on your belly, turning to the left (turn to **342**) or crawl back the way you have come (turn to **333**)?

As you step out from behind trees you remember the words which Glaivas the Ranger spoke to you on the fair ship *Aquamarin*. The city of Doomover is ruled by the Legion of the Sword of Doom who worship the war god, Vasch-Ro, He who sows for the Reaper. Their Marshal, Honoric, is a black-heart who has never been defeated in combat. 'It is said that he once slew a Storm Giant, single-handed. He is without doubt a peerless swordsman.'

Honoric must have been told of your presence by those who saw you near the Ring of Vasch-Ro, unless, you reflect, the gods of evil have sent him to defeat you. You hail him by name and the warrior dismounts and approaches, his great

sword, Sorcerak, swinging from his hip. 'I despise you, ninja, a common assassin who seeks to kill enemies while they sleep. It is only my sense of honour and the sure knowledge that I must triumph over you that prompts me to soil Sorcerak with your blood.'

If you send a shuriken spinning toward the arrogant Marshal's face, turn to **397**. If you have the skill of Poison Needles and wish to use one, turn to **384**. If you choose to rely on your prowess at unarmed combat, turn to **373**.

406

Your fist slams into the back of his neck with deadly precision. There is a loud crack as his neck breaks and he pitches forward spread-eagled on the ground. You have killed the Weaponmaster with a single blow! You kneel down and search his body. Amongst his weapons you find two bottles. One is filled with a green liquid and it is a Potion of Healing. You may drink it at any time and regain up to 10 points of lost Endurance. The other is filled with a blue liquid and is labelled 'Waters of Protection from Ethereal Flame'. Note these on your Character Sheet. Shouldering Aiguchi's body you take it with you through the Victor's Gate. Beyond the Gate is a small hut. As you approach it, Maak emerges hurriedly, but pulls up with a look of disappointment on his face as he sees who is dead and who still lives. 'I see you triumphed once again, ninja,' he says angrily. 'By the laws of the Ring you are now free to go. But once you have left this place you will be fair game for your enemies once more. And you have many enemies, ninja.' With that he turns on his heel and walks into the hut. You leave the body of Aiguchi outside the hut and run on, heading for Irsmuncast. Turn to **416**.

407

As you are passing a run-down pottery factory you notice that the casual stance of one of the idling potters is feigned. Instead of dreaming of better days, his eyes are taking in every detail of your face, as if committing your features to memory. You travel on, betraying no sign that you have noticed this attention, but as soon as you round the corner you peer through one of the cracked quartz windows into the potter's workplace. A small statuette, hidden away in an alcove where no normal man could spot it, catches your eye. It is the effigy of a figure in a quilted black leather jerkin, tight black velvet trousers and executioner's hood. It has four arms, each bearing an object, from a crossbow in one hand to a small black box in the fourth. It is the likeness of the god Torremalku the Slayer, swift-sure bringer of death to beggar and king. You have stumbled across the Assassins' Guild of Tor. You hurry on down Temple Street and push open the wrought-iron gate that surrounds a beautiful but wayward looking garden, a haven of nature in the busy city. The figure of Glaivas is framed in the doorway. Turn to **381**.

408

You must fight yourself. Your double has the same Modifiers, Endurance, Inner Force and items as you do at this moment. Whether or not you punch, kick or throw, your duplicate answers your attack with exactly the same move. If you manage to throw it successfully, you will add 2 to your Punch or Kick Modifier and damage for your next attack. Of course, once your attack is over it will attempt to throw you, and it will mimic your most recent punch or kick if it succeeds. Your double's Defence is 7 against all your attacks, and your Defence against its attacks is also 7. If you successfully hit your double it will always attempt to block the attack. The skill of Yubi-Jutsu will not help you against so canny an opponent. If you win, turn to **390**.

409

The balmy air feels oppressive but your heartfelt prayer is answered. You hear the voice of the Spirit Tiger inside your head. She tells you that the Golem, Everyman, must be killed a hundred times before it is destroyed. If your other plans come to nought you must lure it to the edge of the Bowels of Orb, the Rift which leads to the centre of Orb and from which much of the evil of the world comes forth, and somehow topple the Golem into that chasm. Only then will the enchantment which forces it to try to kill you be broken. Then there is silence. You send up a prayer of thanks to Kwon and to his servant and rise to your feet once more in time to hear the thud, thud of the monster's footsteps as it approaches.

Will you lead it to the Bowels of Orb (turn to **379**) or turn south, hoping that it will fall to its destruction trying to climb after you up one of the peaks (turn to **357**)?

410

The Usurper's men hold firm and a purple standard is carried up the main street. Golspiel's mercenaries, led by Antocidas the One-Eyed have joined the battle before the Palace against you. The mercenaries and the Usurper's soldiers win the day, and the monks of Kwon are slaughtered. You have been spotted and there is no escape from the tower so you climb to the battlement and cast yourself off into the air. Your body is broken on the grass below.

411

Too exhausted to go on, you wait, taking what rest you can. At every moment you expect to see the knotted fists of the Golem as it levers itself back over the lip of the chasm, but hours pass and it does not reappear. At last you crawl away into a shallow pit filled with warm sand to take your first sleep for days.

Turn to **350**.

412

Astaroth's flesh glows fiery red, and when you strike him a numbing smart jolts your limb. Lose 2 Endurance, unless you are wearing the Saint's Locket, in which case you lose but 1 Endurance. Your blows do not have the same effect on Astaroth, seventh Duke of Hell as on men or beasts. If you live, he takes only half of the damage which you inflict, rounding up any fraction. If you chopped at him, turn back to **260** and read on. If you kicked, turn back to **267** and read on.

The balmy air feels oppressive. No-one answers your heartfelt prayer. Will you climb to the hilltop shrine (turn to **360**), double back on yourself in a wide arc towards the Temple to Kwon in the city of Mortavalon (turn to **387**) or head south to the Mountains of Horn, hoping that the monster will fall to its destruction there (turn to **357**)?

As you leave the green gloom of the forest behind you, warmed by bright sunlight, you see, in the distance, gentle rolling hills golden with ripening corn. A river valley runs south-east away from you, towards an anvil-shaped pall of black cloud. 'Do not be deceived by the tamed beauty of the hills,' says Glaivas. 'That corn will feed only slaves. We cannot scale the mountains to the north; we must use guile and stealth to cross these accursed lands. From this point be on your guard against Halvorcs, Orcs, the Priests of Death and,' he drops his voice a shade, 'Ganarre! That cloud hangs over the city called the Walls of Shadow. Only those steeped in evil live there. It is one of the few cities from which every last mission-chapel of the gods of good have been driven forth.' Glaivas says little more and you walk on in silence. You are about to ask who or what is Ganarre, when you reach the banks of the small river. Cresting the hill beyond is a high hedge. Glaivas calls it the Palisade of Thorns and you must scale it or detour many miles. Turn to **404**.

Carefully you draw out a shuriken and take aim. At this range and at an unmoving, unsuspecting target, you cannot miss as you send it whirring towards Aiguchi. It takes him in the shoulder and he spins around, crying out in pain. Roll one die and note that he has lost the result from his Endurance of 15. He glares at you balefully. 'Impressive, ninja. You did well to get so far,' he rasps through gritted teeth. 'But not good enough, for I am a Master of Weapons!' and he throws down his bow and quiver and picks up his curve-bladed spear, the naginata. He then executes a mind-boggling series of movements, as if he were fighting several opponents at once. The naginata is almost a blur as he thrusts and parries, performing a complex but deadly dance. You can see that he is very, very fast, but is he as fast as you? Then he begins to edge towards you, crab-like, the tip of his spear always pointed, unerringly, at your throat. You circle each other. Suddenly he hops and thrusts the spear at your belly with great speed, but you sweep it aside with your arm. For a brief moment you are inside the reach of the naginata. If you have the skill of Yubi-Jutsu, you realise he is too quick for you to use a precision nerve-strike, and you will have to slow him down first. Will you try the Leaping Tiger kick (turn to **56**), the Teeth of the Tiger throw (turn to **22**), a Tiger's Paw chop (turn to **38**) or wait for a suitable moment and, using Inner Force, attempt to snap Aiguchi's naginata (turn to **10**)?

416

You traverse the Barrow Swales, the rolling downs south-east of Mortavalon, at a cautious pace, taking care never to cross the skyline. Thoughts of the Weaponmaster are disturbed by a challenging shout which sends a flock of starlings wheeling into the air. Dropping to one knee behind a stand of trees, you look back to see a magnificent warhorse caparisoned in black and silver. It is still some way away, but its rider's voice sounds chilling and clear. 'Ninja! Show yourself to me. I challenge you to mortal combat. As you reverence Kwon the Babbler of Half-Truths you cannot refuse my challenge. Ninja! Show yourself.'

As the rider approaches, your worst fears are confirmed. He is a great roaring bull of a man, with a three-horned helmet and studded armour. It is Honoric, the Marshal of the Legion of the Sword of Doom, he whom you had thought dead by your own hand but who survived even the Blood of Nil. You may have succeeded in your mission to kill Yaemon that day, but your work is not done while evil men like this still live. You must now kill Honoric in single combat.

Turn to **405**.

417

As you walk back to the Green, you see a family screaming in terror as they are dragged from their homes by orcish soldiers. Their neighbors pelt the soldiers with bricks as they take the poor people away. The crows fly up from the now hideously disfigured bodies stretched and broken on the wheels by the park gates. The High Grandmaster meets you inside the Temple and you tell him that you are firm in your resolve to depose the Usurper. The Grandmaster seems more optimistic and he tells you that a soothsayer whose predictions often come to pass has left a message for you. You must enter the dungeons below the Palace. There you will find something that will aid you to kill the Usurper inside the tomb of the long-dead Overlord Telmain III. You spend next day pondering how to drum up support for the struggle. Which faction will you try to speak to first, the Temple to Time (turn to **394**), the Swordswomen of Dama, Shieldmaiden of the Gods (turn to **296**) or the merchants in their emporia (turn to **184**), or will you try to kindle the rabble (turn to **68**)?

418

You do not feel like singing a song of happiness, held by the grisly Fiend six feet off the ground. But Glaivas starts to sing a merry jig, and you manage to follow suit. The Fiend throws you to the ground but its spell is broken and you dive swiftly aside from its killing blow which buries its horn-tipped arm a foot into the ground. Glaivas' sword is at the ready. Will you attack the Fiend with him (turn to **218**) or flee, leaving the ranger to fight it out (turn to **201**)?

419

The steady beating of the rain on the tree-tops lulls you to sleep, only to dream again of the evil gods and their hatred of you. Once more you see the hawk-faced figure. Its eyes are black and its skin silver. It is Nemesis, Lord of the Cleansing Fire, the Supreme Principle of Evil. Before the god the black cauldron bubbles and the loathsome Fiend bursts from beneath the surface and looks at you. Its eyes are hooded

and black, its face glistens silver in the moonlight, it has no mouth and chin. Instead of hands it has two spikes of bone, like blunted horns. Suddenly, it spreads huge black leathery wings and launches its bulk into the night. You know that it is coming for you.

You wake with a start to a thrill of fear. You can hear nothing, but you know something is wrong. Glaivas stands stock still, on watch. He seems on edge and you cannot hear any of the night sounds that should fill the forest. An unnatural chill gust of wind whips the leaves into a whirlpool before you, and Glaivas starts uneasily.

Will you eat the mandrake root and try to call the Spirit Tiger (turn to **104**), launch yourself into a Winged Horse kick at the whirlpool (turn to **116**) or walk towards Glaivas and wait to see what happens (turn to **128**)?

420

The tide of battle has turned in your favour. As the Usurper's Halvorc guards fall back towards the Palace gates, it seems everyone has declared for you. The shieldmaidens make a determined attack and the rabble pelts the Halvorcs with bricks and spears. Golspiel's mercenaries arrive as the monks of Kwon scale the walls of the Palace gardens. Only the priests of Time do not take to the streets in your support. Seeing that there is no hope left, the Palace guard surrenders and the Force-Lady Gwyneth orders them to be confined to barracks, after they have lain down their swords. You walk down the stairs of the tower and out into the garden and a great cheer goes up as the rapturous crowd recognises you. 'Behold your new Overlord, Avenger!' cries the High Grandmaster of the Temple to Kwon.

At evening that day you are seated in the Throne Room of the Palace. Your father's flag flies proudly once again where, until today, that of the Usurper had flown. Force-Lady Gwyneth raises the rose-crown of Irsmuncast and hands it to the High Grandmaster. Bowing your head, you give thanks to Kwon as he sets the crown on your brow, saying 'I crown thee, Avenger, Overlord of the city state of Irsmuncast nigh Edge, Protector of the Manmarch against the Rift.' A cheer echoes round the Throne Room, but the people ₌eering you are all strangers. You put a brave face on it. As you process onto the balcony and the crowd screams its adulation you reflect that the days ahead will be a true test of your wisdom. Can you sow the seeds of good government in a city of religious schisms, racial tensions, unscrupulous greed and warring factions with proud leaders? Only time will tell in what could be your greatest challenge yet.

Continued in the Way of the Tiger 4: OVERLORD!